WHAT BOOKS PRESS

AN IMPRINT OF

THE GLASS TABLE

COLLECTIVE

LOS ANGELES

ALSO BY FORREST ROTH

Line and Pause
The Sullen Pages (chapbook)

GARY OLDMAN IS
A BUILDING YOU MUST
WALK THROUGH

FORREST ROTH

WHAT
BOOKS
PRESS

LOS ANGELES

Publisher's Cataloging-In-Publication Data

Names: Roth, Forrest.

Title: Gary Oldman is a building you must walk through / Forrest Roth.

Description: Los Angeles : What Books Press, [2017]

Identifiers: ISBN 978-0-9962276-6-7

Subjects: LCSH: Sid and Nancy (Motion picture)--Fiction. | Rock musicians--Fiction. | Los Angeles (Calif.)--Fiction.

Classification: LCC PS3618.O84 G37 2017 | DDC 813/.6--dc23

Cover art: Gronk, *untitled*, mixed media on paper, 2016
Book design by Ash Good, www.ashgood.design

What Books Press
363 South Topanga Canyon Boulevard
Topanga, CA 90290

WHATBOOKSPRESS.COM

GARY OLDMAN IS
A BUILDING YOU MUST
WALK THROUGH

CONTENTS

PROLOGUE:
BECAUSE YOU AND YOU ALL WANTED
A PROLOGUE FOR WHATEVER REASON

IT HAD OCCURRED

to me it occurred, let me really say, had the occurring I speak of otherwise would be something, someone other if not I, a something, a someone to you and you all should I occur before this occurring, I initially at farthest possible distance only to come closer, at creeping speed as it were, until I have the distance to be seen by you, and you all—enough for a trace, an outline, and outlier even—and, being seen this way, it occurs to you and you all I am something or someone first though only unto myself, a shape with no shape, a flimsy idea, a terrible disappointment, a vaguest looking-at until the distance presents itself now as something, someone I would be other than myself should the distance close considerably but only upon my own consideration of my own looming, my own occurring (which, by the way, no, still hasn't occurred yet) and then leaving at a point unseen by everyone and no one as all distance leaves so a someone may take note that the leavings left keep but a day, whereupon you and you all feel a wash of gentleness pass over as this limit occurs without me.

I have to tell you and you all there will be a day.

You and you all will require knowing what kind of a day it will be, yet I think all days can't be qualified so accurately. I resist. You and you all insist. My choices are severely limited by this insistence. Is not a day enough. No, you and you all say. A day must mean something. Something must happen to make it mean something. I must make it happen. No one else. This seems dire, but that's the point, I am told. I did not intend to make it dire, this occurring. I did not intend to make any occurring anything. That's the point, I say. A day intends nothing. A limit is only myself predicated upon so many conditions. Too many. Why make this difficult. You and you all and I. Who else. What else. What more is needed. I think you and you all understand. I am not so sure now. Once I used to be sure, but something occurred, whatever it was. It wasn't me, that's for certain. Someone else made that happen. The I, most likely. Also not me. Still, you and you all insist. Wanting. Needing. It can't just be the I. A single occurrence is not enough. Never enough. There has to be more, much more, many more. There are so many days needing to be filled because of this occurring that it would be unthinkable for me to speak in terms of the solitary, the isolated, the meaningless. A grain of sand buried in the desert. A single wave drowning in the ocean. A leaf left hanging on the tree. You and you all refuse. You and you all can't have this. Voices are raised. Protests are organized. Threats are suggested. Deaths are accomplished. And the lessons taught. The gentleness turns into something other than gentleness, as it usually does, only when no one is aware of the turning. That's what the desire of knowing a day gets you and you all in the end. Paying attention to these things would be advisable. Don't say later I didn't give any warning, even if I haven't yet.

There may be an actual story occurring somewhere here in this elaboration. Yes, I am growing aware of it, I think. I am now convoluting the I.

Consider this while I keep occurring to myself.

Let me really say the occurring I decide to compromise with with you and you all in the fervent hope I will occur (for whatever personal benefit that entails may be determined afterwards) will indeed occur. I will give you and you all what you want. What you need. What you demand. But something has to occur in return. It is only fair. Even if it is unexpected. That's what it means to be gentle. You and you all have to be gentle. Everyone. No exceptions. Yes, there have been exceptions, many of them, but you and you all know they do not count. They can't be tolerated, enjoyable as they may be. Gentleness is what we want, including those who are never gentle and never care for gentleness. I will have to remind everyone of the threats made against me in case you and you all have forgotten already. Don't worry, however. I will always be gentle about it. Even when I am not gentle. It is part of our strange little deal. No need to thank me so soon. No need to thank me at all.

A solitary, isolated, but not altogether meaningless day, then.

I will make it a day, before I die in any sense of the word or experience something like what I think my death will resemble to other people, where all the gentle men and gentle women of this gentle world point and laugh at me in public for the sake of an etiquette which has failed because no one is aware of it. It has the air of foreboding, this day. The sense that everything gentle is about to be turned upside down in some fashion until it is no longer gentle. Since this day has almost occurred, the concern here is whether anyone will recognize this particular quality of this specific day when it happens since I am hardly any concern whatsoever to anyone, especially anyone who is gentle. That may change later, however. For whatever reason, I doubt it at present. Hence, the foreboding you and you all are suffering here. I can be blamed for that.

In the ever-opening open space of a solitary, isolated, but not altogether meaningless day, I let you and you all see myself sitting and reading a book, one of the most accessible visual clues of any story and all stories materializing in an observer's perception. It may not be a book I particularly care for, but it will be an actual book with actual pages of actual paper which I fervently, passionately, but not outwardly hope contains an actual story—something I haven't written myself, least of all for a novel—though I already know I will ruin this story by thinking that it exists only to entertain me or edify me or a combination of both, even as I serve to entertain or edify or do both for all the gentle people around me, my more immediate performance for them being to serve as the object of ridicule for my obsolescence in the latest personal technology if not my literary tastes.

Or, if it won't be me, then someone else. Someone else will be reading the last actual book in the world while surrounded by the preternatural glow of illuminated faces above incandescent crotches. Someone else dealing with the ridicule of limit in the ever-opening open space. Someone else subjected to gentle people who are no longer gentle and are unaware of it despite the favorable compromise offered just now with fairly generous terms, as I see it, at least.

For the love of geedee please, I beg, let all this occur to someone else.

Because I fear myself in the occurring—more so than other people, gentle or not. I do not want to be clear. I am no philosopher. I am no martyr. I can't stand the thought of being pointed at and laughed at out of politeness as I, with earliest personal technology, read an actual book, out of all the pressing thoughts I could ever stand for myself. I can't be blamed for that. It is not my fault but the fault of finality. Being this gentle forever. In this particular story, which I have yet to write, I can't give up actual books because it occurs to me this day that someone has to be the last reader. Always there may not be a someone else after me even if there actually is. The principle of extinction works as such, from Dodo birds to Mohicans to important American movies. This nobility of scarce preciousness. Though I am anything but noble. Though I recognize anything but nobility, especially in everyone else while gentleness abounds. The burdens of occurring, I say, finally. Until the occurring stops. If it ever does.

I sense the I needs to work this out some more with you and you all. I hope you and you all will be satisfied with this particular day asked for. It is difficult to create more than one day, should you and you all not be satisfied (I'm counting on that), but there may be a way for another to happen.

It becomes imperative there must be an I who is forever someone else to everyone else, then, an I who is a day occurring to me as I sit and read while a television is on, while a gentle conversation is taking place, while someone else pretends they are everyone else who is not me occurring to someone else—least of all you and you all—before the blinds in this room are drawn, blinding no one—least of all the I occurring now—which does not occur to those who pull blinds, thinking I have not seen the day end before I have ended myself and, as this occurs to me, the someone else to everyone else that I am knows all of this day and yet could never make it all occur to you and you all outside this room, outside this building, where etiquette is played with forever as though it were a hallway winding and spelling until a door that occurs to me is what I point towards, it pointing towards you and you all, saying, I cannot be this I.

An I who is forever something and someone else to everyone else in some finality, no matter how remote, even if no one sympathetic or recognizable or likable or merely gentle.

In shorter words: I welcome myself to this prologue for you and you all.

Right. Now kindly piss off.

YOUR FAMOUS SISTER WALKING THROUGH A PLATE-GLASS DOOR AT THE GEHRY MUSEUM IF IT EXISTED

I DISTRUST PEOPLE, everyone in this city, those who speak in the anecdotal.

Yes I know you did something. We all did. And we all know each other. We all know your famous sister, and you and her were, like,

aberrant: seeming to cause willful self-injury and thus a seething insult. A building in any city.

When we went away to collect your famous sister in Los Angeles and bring her back here again, I knew you were mentally distancing yourself along with me from the facility we entered, a nondescript medical building shaped in the way medical buildings today are shaped as the means to avoid the accident of trying to walk through it unscathed, like your famous sister deliberately walking through a plate-glass door by trying to imitate Gary Oldman as Sid Vicious from Alex Cox's 1986 film *Sid and Nancy*. This had been coming for several years, and you had been a part of it. Women don't walk through plate-glass doors, she had told me, only men like Gary Oldman do. Then she finally does it herself, though not very well at all, and while putting down the phone you were, like, hey. I know, I know. I already knew your famous sister wasn't good for the full ride. She only put some of her arm through, the gentle people at nondescript medical building told us, barely brushing the handle on the other side until jerking herself back and the security men stepping in. You and I spent a couple of hours sitting on the sidewalk in Los Angeles thinking about it and her. But not anecdotally if we could help it.

Another event soon becoming just another toxicological. Residual pealing mirth of your famous sister's stare, one eyebrow raised, and the next. Indistinguishable from yours. A few months ago we travelled to your civil servant parents' home upstate at your insistence, and they did not want to recognize me but you were, like, Here he is. And I am, now. An aberration. An instruction. Attempting conversation, I asked your demure mother about movies, which both avoided and did not avoid conversation about your famous sister. Mothers, I find, do not usually know *Sid and Nancy*. Mothers do not know your famous sister, which include yours. Your father, well, it was another day. Another event, like, your civil servant parents are a building I keep walking through. I spent a few minutes barely on the handle on the other side, your famous sister said. Don't walk through it—run. Your sister always thought she was too good for your civil servant parents, and upstate in general. Those were two things in particular I have liked about her.

In this trivial way you had recognized me again. I had moved back into our place in the aberrant, self-loathing city, waiting for you on the sofa, your own discharge, but not your famous sister as you had accused me of with some reasonable accuracy. One eyebrow raised. Falling through. It was your birthday. You wanted me to do impersonations to celebrate. Men do not fall through. Men do not imitate Gary Oldman as Sid Vicious from *Sid and Nancy*. Yet your famous sister has said Gary Oldman is a building we all must keep walking through. The plate-glass of his face is meant to cause an accident, which I should do aberrant, instructively, but not anecdotally. Your civil servant parents were, like, security on the other side. I like your parents as long as I can put my arm through them. I distrust men especially, and your famous sister. I distrust the Gehry Museum in Los Angeles. Gary Oldman has been to Los Angeles countless occasions, but your famous sister only twice, and neither have been to the Gehry Museum. No one has ever been to the Gehry Museum. It is a willful self-injury and thus a seething insult to your civil servant parents who know better. I think they are charming. I want to put my arm through them, step in, and brush the familial mirth of you and your famous sister during the 1980's. I want to understand them and her and you as an event, as, like, an aberration but not an anecdote

so you were, like,

how could I be an imitation of Gary Oldman which all men would hate me for. Gary Oldman could kill me with his face, but I say you can't with yours. Your face is, like, a small event. An endless toxicology. An endless building that an important author who understands buildings like Maurice Blanchot can make for Gary Oldman, but Gary Oldman will not read anything because, like, he is too busy going to the Los Angeles in his mind where the Gehry Museum only exists, according to your famous sister. The Gehry Museum of Gary Oldman's mind, she says, is only made of plate-glass doors which Sid Vicious continually walks through, thinking he is Gary Oldman before Gary Oldman met her. The pealing mirth of you returning home. A while back you started recognizing my eyebrows with your finger, which also met with the gentle women who do not know your famous sister. I know I am thinking about her right now. Thinking about your civil servant parents who gave me exactly three lukewarm dinners of canned ham, canned peas and reconstituted mashed potatoes on paper plates, as though they were trying to prevent an accident. Before that, they were too good for me. Before that, you moved back into our place and meant to brush my eyebrows while I slept, and then we were supposed to travel everywhere that was not Los Angeles, forgetting your famous sister and speaking as though only you and I would recognize each other in this world. On instinct tonight while you are sleeping I keep talking to your famous sister as though I am Gary Oldman, aberrantly, instructively, but not anecdotally, a plate-glass door I keep trying to walk into and being escorted out by security men at the Gehry Museum because the Gehry Museum is too good for me despite that it does not exist. I keep trying to walk into it because I know she will be gone by tomorrow morning or some other morning. Because your civil servant parents want the best for all of us, which is not the Gehry Museum. They want for us the building made by a Maurice Blanchot which does not have plate-glass windows but ten thousand eyebrows instead. Which does not have your famous sister. Your famous sister who, like, met Gary Oldman

you were, like, oh my god, like, no fucking way

but yes it was the fucking way indeed which meets you returning home. Yes. Like, I was, like, your famous sister who went through Los Angeles and moved back in with us for only a single night. Everywhere I am meant to be. Everywhere I keep trying to walk through with you because you mean well despite your famous sister who keeps walking into plate-glass doors at buildings that are not the Gehry Museum, because before you and her were discharged it was, like, her dream to walk through a plate-glass door at the Gehry Museum in Los Angeles like she was, like, Sid Vicious even though Sid Vicious never went to the Gehry Museum because Gary Oldman is composed of ten thousand eyebrows which cannot get past security and, like, Los Angeles, no fucking way, and you were like

oh my god

oh my god

your famous sister forever tries meeting you in a building meant to cause an accident

me sleeping through your imitation of her Gary Oldman

sharing with me the anecdotes of all the famous actors your famous sister worked with in the 1980's before you were discharged as I see their faces as you see them always meeting you in the hallway, sitting down to dinner with you in the dinner place as you share food with them, best utensils out, and you tell them, like, Gary Oldman really was Sid Vicious in *Sid and Nancy* and that really was a plate-glass door your sister walked through just like the instructive Sid Vicious because she thought he was aberrant in real life but this is now aberrant in Gary Oldman's way, the door she walked through and her blood brushed her hand to the floor before security arrived and put her in with all the famous actors she worked with in the 1980's before you were discharged, including the ones who worked with Maurice Blanchot while he designed the Gehry Museum to infuriate your civil servant parents and let your famous sister move out, like she was always meeting you in the hallway with the women who did not know your famous sister before she walked through the plate-glass door at the Gehry Museum which does not exist because she met the Gary Oldman who was not you, because I wake up with you on me and I'm, like, no way, I know

I did something. I know I had said to you we should do something about her, go somewhere other than the Los Angeles of your mind where all the famous actors of the 1980's are not, which would be in Gary Oldman's mind where your sister does not reside with her countless city ur-friends with endless anecdotes, not stories, wishing I could find a cup of coffee somewhere with you, without anyone I know or do not know so I could pull up to someone and say, This is her

story is, story goes, like, your famous sister said hey to Gary Oldman on the sidewalk while her hand was bleeding from putting it through a plate-glass window at the Gehry Museum if it existed, and while waiting for security to arrive Gary Oldman asked if she was okay and had someone called an ambulance like they did for Sid Vicious which she thought was really sweet of him and she was falling in love with the Gary Oldman circa *Sid and Nancy* even though that day Gary Oldman had a moustache and his Sid Vicious had been relatively hairless with the exception of his spiky head hair, but he talked to her calmly, gently, even instructively, telling her how to control the bleeding as if he forgot who he was even though she didn't and would have bled all over the sidewalk to continue gazing at Gary Oldman and him talking to her and him signing her AUTOGRAPHS book which she had thought would make a fine story but not an anecdote other than the security men arriving before the ambulance, by then Gary Oldman being long gone, pushed along by another person with him, an ur-friend, or probably his agent who had no facial hair and no head hair and did not bother with ambulances in Los Angeles because they were only poor anecdotal devices, forever to be mistrusted and avoided with the seething intensity of Gary Oldman as Sid Vicious when he kills Nancy Spungen with a knife which Gary Oldman left as either an intentional act or a complete accident which had struck your famous sister as rather sublime when she watched *Sid and Nancy* at sixteen, romantic, instructive, but not anecdotal, not Gary Oldman saying nothing to her as he blithely walked by without helping her on the sidewalk, bleeding.

One night your famous sister shows us her AUTOGRAPHS book. You and I thoughtfully stare at what could be the signature of the Gary Oldman she says she met in Los Angeles, who stopped to help and talk to her. It is more clean and determined than what you or I would expect of someone who had captured the essence of Sid Vicious to be, particularly the expansive O, playful, inviting, contrasting the secured, mature masculinity of a refined, well-aged Gary Oldman. Sid Vicious most likely had the signature of a third grader. You and I have never seen his signature for ourselves. As likely no one else ever did. I am one of those people who put much stock in signatures as a designator of an intelligence quotient relative to the signer's appreciation of general aesthetics. I am embarrassed for the person who signs a weak signature in front of me. I had spent countless hours in our upstate high school working on mine instead of calculus. When I first saw your famous sister's signature in front of me, signing a receipt for a dinner she could not pay for, I wondered how she became so famous to begin with, though before I said something about it I caught myself, thinking it was only slightly worse than yours. I am embarrassed being in your company when you sign such a signature. I admit it. I do not care that your writing in general is not terribly interesting, as is your sister's, but only that there was not an upper case O like Gary Oldman's which

I could slip myself through and see the other side of you. But your family name does not begin with O. In fact, there are no O's in your name whatsoever, but your famous sister has not one but two of them in her first name, which helps explain the easiness of her popularity when she is not walking through plate-glass doors. Why did your civil servant parents give you a name with no O's but then give your sister two of them. My name has two O's, one in my first name, one in my last name, neither of them upper case. When I sign them out, I think of Gary Oldman and the flair he must put into his upper case O while he is signing it and whether it is the same as when he acts. When he feels like a scene is not happening, perhaps he goes to his dressing room in between takes and writes all these upper case O's over and over until he realizes what a beautiful signature he has.

There is nothing beautiful about your famous sister's signature, you and I both admit. Even Gary Oldman could not make her signature beautiful. Even ten thousand eyebrows could not make her signature beautiful. Even the Gehry Museum in Los Angeles if it existed could not make her signature beautiful. So she believes walking through a plate-glass door there could.

During the 1980's when your famous sister started talking about walking through a plate-glass door, you had to sign her out of discharge since she couldn't sign herself out. A signature in America can be the means to self-release, the familial name the virtual key which turns the lock, except your famous sister had changed her family name to something better suiting her first name with the two O's in it. The pseudonym also has two O's in it, a catchy assonance not unlike my name, which was not intentional, instructive, or anecdotal, but a name that was interesting only because my non-civil servant parents found it interesting. Your famous sister was often ashamed of her signature as a child because yours was much better, she had told me, and in self-conscious shame practiced her handwriting to no end, the beating pulse of her wrist across the paper working her pen over and over until she lost her name under a pile of scribbles, driving the pen through the legal pad. Punishing the paper, punishing herself, hey. Your famous sister does not like to write. If you are a talented actor in Los Angeles, then it is not so important to write. Speaking is everything. Anything else can get a body double. But the only writing you need is an intelligent-looking signature. This could be why Los Angeles does not allow famous actors to write in the cement at Mann's Chinese Theater anymore since writing in wet cement is childish, and childish-looking. The greatest, most talented American actors of the 1980's could not afford to look childish. Gary Oldman, at any point in his life, was never childish. Gary Oldman had to be raised by a violent alcoholic father, something which requires less and less childish behavior as one becomes more of a child to counteract the violent alcoholic tendencies, until, at some point, Gary Oldman takes on colorful roles which require a violent alcoholic personality like Sid Vicious in *Sid and Nancy*. Your famous sister, studying the large of O of Gary Oldman's signature, believes this is the best performance of his career but did not tell him so when she met him in Los Angeles because she was, like, bleeding all over the place and the security men prevented her from reaching out and touching him with blood on her hand. Sid Vicious was the apotheosis of Gary Oldman's storied career and he hasn't been better since, your famous sister says, he's been mostly shit in everything else except maybe *The Professional* but oh my god he's Sid Vicious even when he says, Bore-reen, and how pizza is his favorite food, always Sid Vicious at every conceivable laconic instant especially since Gary Oldman can't play bass guitar but had a violent alcoholic father who surely Sid Vicious' father would have been had Sid Vicious' father actually been present in the life of Sid Vicious, which he was not, and Sid Vicious never saw the signature of his father and probably could not even write his real name or his stage name or the name of his mother or the names of his bandmates or the name of what only Sid Vicious could bring into existence by walking through a plate-glass door, the attribute of Sid Vicious as seen by Gary Oldman raised by a violent alcoholic father by the name of Sid Vicious.

While you are sleeping I go into the living room where your famous sister is trying to sleep on the sofa and tell her Gary Oldman is not a beautiful man, but I concede he has a beautiful signature. I think this is a fair compromise. Your famous sister yells at me. Curses at me. Calls me every filthy name. Says you and I are bore-reen. Threatens to leave us. In this moment, she is a beautiful woman whose signature was the ugliness of trying to walk through a plate-glass door at the Gehry Museum in Los Angeles if it existed while Gary Oldman watched and was reminded of himself as the Sid Vicious who could not sign his own name.

I see Gary Oldman is not as beautiful as your famous sister who could sign her name in wet cement while sleeping if she ever had to.

Your famous sister is, like, so angry at me. Doesn't believe it. Nope.

You and I should not be surprised that we can't impersonate Gary Oldman forever. Maybe she could since she believes she met him.

When you and I read her predictable farewell note to us, scrawled in that childish handwriting, we will then remember she had wanted to sign the ugliness of Mann's Chinese Theater before we got her out of Los Angeles, and be reminded of all the famous actors she knew and would be casted as in the film adaptation of their semi-autobiographical lives. She can do both female and male roles effortlessly, walk through them with the impunity of the Gehry Museum walking through the Los Angeles cityscape if it were ever to exist outside of Gary Oldman's mind the way Mann's Chinese Theater does. In every American city and town there is a Mann's Chinese Theater to compensate for the lack of a Gehry Museum. Mann's Chinese Theater is the most unfortunate aspect of latter-day American existence, causing willful injury and seething insult from its insisting all innocent bystanders must kneel upon the concrete and press their palms into the indentations of those who came before. You found the residual nature of this collective activity to be unhealthy, lame, and, like, totally gross. You and I had no choice in the matter because this is Los Angeles I am talking about. Your famous sister made us press our palms into the indentations and hold them there waiting for the conceivable instant to reach us as it had reached your famous sister who believed she was commiserating with Audrey Hepburn even though she thought Audrey Hepburn was, like, way too petite. She would sooner play

Gary Oldman than Audrey Hepburn. She alone understands Gary Oldman who did not sign his name into the wet cement of Mann's Chinese Theater, who never left his imprint there, because no one who is gentle may access the residue of Gary Oldman superficially, instinctively, or anecdotally.

It can't be that easy. It can never be that easy because this is the Gary Oldman who even Sid Vicious had never become in his own life, who the gentle people in this world try to become but often fail at it. The gentle people must instead take a chance. They must become Sid Vicious being Gary Oldman and try walking through the plate-glass door, and only then may they walk through the building unharmed

I say to you sleeping as if I would know.

FIVE INTRODUCERS AT
A PUBLIC READING FOR SID VICIOUS
AND GARY OLDMAN

A VERY GOOD EVENING to You, and You All, Too—

I would like to welcome you and you all to a public reading for Sid
Vicious and Gary Oldman, except this reading is not happening in a
conventional or contrived sense but is instead made a faulty representation
of one in your mind, as well as in all of the other minds in this non-
attendance. Sid Vicious, as you and you all know well, was the infamous
bassist for the equally infamous British punk band The Sex Pistols despite
lingering questions to this day as to whether he could actually play the
bass guitar, possibly or very likely was the catalyst which drove the band
to break up in the middle of a disastrous American tour, possibly or very
likely murdered his American lover Nancy Spungen at the Hotel Chelsea
in New York City in 1978, most definitely died before seeing trial in
1979, and assuredly was the featured subject of the popular 1986 movie
Sid and Nancy, which is, like, one of your famous sister's most favorite
movies. Sid Vicious was played by Gary Oldman in the film, an actor
who is generally regarded as being a famous, talented, and anecdotal
gentle man with a violent alcoholic past. Sid Vicious, a violent alcoholic
himself, won no awards in his relatively short lifetime, but Gary Oldman
has won many awards in his relatively long career for a violent alcoholic

acting style, including for playing a violent alcoholic Sid Vicious in *Sid and Nancy* who may or may not have murdered Nancy Spungen. Though neither of these men will be present or speaking to you directly in the aforementioned conventional or contrived sense, I am very glad to have both here this evening all the same in your mind, as well as in all of the other minds in voluntary (or less than voluntary) non-attendance. They will be of great help as you mourn the untimely, anticipated, but not anecdotal death of your famous sister in the aberrant, self-loathing city. But not quite yet. This reading not happening is far too important for only one introducer. Let us give our next introducer a big literary welcome, then, shall we. Gentle applause.

Dear Not-Happening Readers—

Once I wanted you beginning. You wanted you all to begin. And you all wanted to begin reading. You all wanted to read a story. A story about a person who was never gentle, unlike yourselves, like Sid Vicious or your famous sister, someone not at all close to me yet whom I may detest and learn to resent with a seething intensity, my emotions disguised under convention and contrivance and a general awe of my being placed before him or her. I would then be introducing a subject of the first and highest order—unlike the previous introducer—and become another narrator with the mastery of a subject enough to put it in the mind's eye and immediacy of my audience, which you all say we are fully due and accorded. An audience is our birthright, our natural expectation to the use of function, our very existence. Even the Puritans knew that. Today everybody forgets they must be an introducer until a Gary Oldman enters their bore-reen, gentle life with a violent alcoholic Sid Vicious who becomes the fascination of a famous sister—in this case, yours. Please remember: I am, like, so not responsible for anything which follows.

I am attempting an introduction because your famous sister, despite her apparent fame, needs introducers herself, and they are as well-deserved as the three lukewarm meals prepared by your civil servant parents in their upstate home when I visit, who will not even speak her name at the table for fear of ruining my appetite in your presence. As an introducer, my appetite cannot be tamed by the absence or presence of names but, like most American audiences, the novelty of them to our lives when they are introduced to us which we play with vicious intensity and aberrant self-denial. We know our lives would be empty without names, especially the famous ones. If I deny mine to you, you may slowly grow to hate me and my semblance of a life as it opens in front of you—assuming it ever does—but as an introducer it is not my name you are concerned about but my subject's instead, and my subject's instead is the withholding of every judgment you place at my feet (if you could see them, that is, since we never care about a narrator's feet, but only his or her or its hands).

All I can say is, every so often, someone reminds the world that even Jesus ate at the tables of prostitutes.

To the Members of the Perpetually Seated Audience—

Instead, I think you and you all will agree, is the best possible thing I can do for you and you all. *Instead* is beautiful, if not always truthful. *Instead* is the greatest consideration America ever invented among its myriad considerations. Instead of being an introducer, we could be Gary Oldman, and often we all are Gary Oldman, the product of a violent alcoholic household which was your particular *instead*, away from the calm upstate civil servant household, you and your famous sister watching movies with Gary Oldman in them—as well as with Molly Ringwald and Tom Hulce and all of the other famous actors of the 1980's she knows—before she is discharged and judgment withheld about her long enough so she could walk though the door, out the building, and into the self-injurious city.

A city, any city, is filled with millions of plate-glass doors today. Many of them are automated, and thus are difficult to deliberately walk through, but a majority are still of manual operation, requiring on occasion a friendly gentle stranger's obsolete gesture to hold it open and observe what is known as proper etiquette. No one ever held a door open for Sid Vicious in real life, and there were not many automatic doors at that particular Time, if I am not mistaken. It was not an accident, then, that the real Sid Vicious and Gary Oldman as Sid Vicious in *Sid and Nancy* walked through a plate-glass door, distracted by someone calling out what he thought was his name, but an act of revolt against civilized society's true lack of etiquette, or, I should say, the pretense of etiquette which constitutes any building in any city. But I am not Sid Vicious, nor am I Gary Oldman playing Sid Vicious in *Sid and Nancy*. I am someone who holds and has held open plate-glass doors for a countless number of gentle strangers who I never see again as they disappear into etiquette, into the vast, unknowable building of Gary Oldman's America.

Your famous sister is somewhere in one of these buildings where someone— maybe or especially a gentle man—holds open a plate-glass door for her, carefully, firmly, but not anecdotally. This gentle man, all the same, follows her inside. He is entranced by the sour look she gives him because she has been thwarted by etiquette and is now inside the building without going through a plate-glass door like Sid Vicious, lost, not wanting to be here under these conditions. Since he knows he belongs in that building at least and knows it very well, he feels he has a certain claim to its purpose, its outlay, its overall aesthetic harmony of making someone not feel lost— unlike, for instance, the buildings of Maurice Blanchot—and so asks her where she is going and could he be of any assistance in finding her destination. Instead of answering she ignores him completely, fully, but rudely, and she looks for a staircase, finds it, begins making a long ascent up twelve flights despite the working elevators being the more preferable ascending option, which strikes him as odd because gentle men will always take an elevator with gentle women. He wonders if she is not really a gentle woman but someone like Nancy Spungen instead, the kind of *instead* woman he has never known but perhaps had thought about after turning off *Sid and Nancy* halfway through because the movie disgusted him. He had not felt the deep appreciation of Gary Oldman that he does now after a long acting career of winning many awards for many notable roles which did not involve saving women—especially prostitutes and Puritan adulterers—until fairly recently.

You know, the one where he bounds up the stairs at the end of the movie to save the woman he loves, even after finding out she was selling herself to other men, before she threw herself off the building because she believed firmly, truly, but not effortlessly that no one—particularly whoever Gary Oldman was playing—loved her and that she would never be anything more than a prostitute in a building in any city.

You know, that one. Not the psychopathic murderous DEA agent versus the invincible Italian pedophile assassin one, the other one. Though that movie works here, too, because often you all will never know for certain who should save your children from adolescence.

May I Ever Have Your Attention, Please—

The real Nancy Spungen was known to enter buildings in conventional
ways because it was unlikely a gentle man or gentle woman would
hold open doors for her in public. Your famous sister already differs
from Nancy Spungen in this respect. Your famous sister, unlike Nancy
Spungen, has been to Mann's Chinese Theater to put her hands into the
famous concrete hand prints and would have gone to the Gehry Museum
in Los Angeles if it actually existed outside of Gary Oldman's mind.
Like Nancy Spungen, your famous sister shows a preference for stairs,
especially when they lead to the rooftop of a building where most gentle
people seldom go when they enter a building. Your famous sister often
dares to tread where most gentle people do not—that is why, of course,
she is famous, other than starring in movies with the famous American
actors of the 1980's. Some people become famous in America for falling
into a coma, others for jumping off a tall building. This is not the sort
of fame your famous sister seeks, I know, because your famous sister
means to rearrange the social order of American etiquette as Sid Vicious
would have surely done had he not killed Nancy Spungen at the Hotel
Chelsea—accidentally or otherwise—and then OD'd later. He would
have failed better by merely stumbling off the roof of a tall building after
taking a final swig of vodka, a tempting theory your famous sister may be
willing to consider since she has no idea what she is doing right now in
this building.

It has been said, or at least intonated, by many Nobel Prize-winning
authors that a gentle man will not let a gentle woman fall to her death,
much less deliberately walk through a plate-glass door. Because he never
finished watching *Sid and Nancy*, this gentle man is unsure of that. Some
people deserve to walk through a plate-glass door or throw themselves
off a tall building, yet no Nobel Prize-winning author has ever suggested
this. To be sure, there are many more people than these in America
who deserve to walk up twelve flights of stairs, even when the elevators
are working, but the gentle man is not certain whether your famous
sister is one of them. Even if she does bear some resemblance to Nancy
Spungen. He himself bears no resemblance to Sid Vicious or even Gary

Oldman as Sid Vicious or even the real Gary Oldman who was raised in a violent alcoholic household. He is just another nameless, faceless gentle man following your famous sister up the stairs carefully, quietly, but not constructively, making sure that she does not see him but, while this is happening, she is aware that someone else is indeed in the stairwell and may possibly, potentially, but not innocently follow her up to the roof where something anecdotal may happen but in all likelihood nothing will happen, which is what usually happens in most American buildings you and I never seem to avoid, as well as what usually happens to Nobel Prize-winning authors who visit Niagara Falls or less famous ones who stay at the famous Hotel Chelsea for no particular reason other than wanting to stay at the famous Hotel Chelsea.

To Those Perhaps Deserving of Death—

On this special occasion tonight, I am so humbled and very pleased to introduce you to the two people who have never thrown themselves off the rooftop of a building: one who belonged in the building in question, and one who did not in the conventional and contrived sense of *belonging* somewhere—namely, of having a building anticipate your famous sister's presence. This is a strange thing to consider, but we must consider it all the same because I am introducing it. Without this introduction you all would have no idea what I am talking about, which is the only unacceptable development when speaking anecdotally. You all must know who is being dealt with here because how will you all sit still otherwise and not want to walk through a plate-glass door without hurting yourself. You all will sit still only when the one who makes the introduction is finished with the introduction and lets us watch two people who do not know the other throw themselves off a building because they could never walk through a plate-glass door in our reality of etiquette which does not belong to Sid Vicious or Gary Oldman as Sid Vicious. But you all soon learn Sid Vicious does not introduce our reality because it is Gary Oldman who is a building we must walk through, even if, like the gentle man, we turn off *Sid and Nancy* halfway through because we are disgusted with the fictional counterparts of Sid Vicious and Nancy Spungen or the real-life counterparts we ourselves could become if we get the introduction of a gentle man who follows your famous sister to the roof of building he works at and feels impelled to save her only because he has to save himself in the process lest he follow her off the rooftop. At the very least, if he survives and she instead falls, it will make for a good anecdote, his optimistic self rationalizes. He starts wondering whether your famous sister is in her right mind and if she is anything like the real Nancy Spungen, someone who was not a gentle woman but perhaps did not deserve to die even if she deserved to climb twelve flights of stairs while the elevators were still working.

To make himself absolutely sure of this fact, he talks your famous sister out of an imminent suicide pact, walks back down twelve flights of stairs with her, rents *Sid and Nancy* at her recommendation from the last remaining video store in the city with a VHS section, returns to his very

comfortable apartment with her, dusts off his video player, and decides
to finally watch the disturbing second half of the movie, turning to your
famous sister sitting next to him on his very comfortable leather sofa with
voluminous tears in her eyes during the final implied afterlife reunion and
the very touching music and the triumphant end credits and saying to
her, You know you didn't really deserve to die.

THE SIGNATURE OF A GENTLE MAN
AS SID VICIOUS

YOU AND I STARE at the signature of the Gary Oldman your famous
sister met in Los Angeles. That is: the handwriting your famous sister procured
with or without the real Gary Oldman, which, at first glance, appears to be
independent of an ordinary human hand—if there was, in fact, a hand at
all signing and not the sheer force of violent alcoholic intensity which Gary
Oldman the famous actor is known for and has harnessed so well in playing,
for instance, Sid Vicious in *Sid and Nancy*, a famous role allowing him later
to project a semi-autonomous discursive apparatus that constructs a standard
handwritten indicator of the subject's name, this particular one induced by
your famous sister's modest request while she was bleeding in front of the
Gehry Museum if, in fact, it actually exists. Needless to say, the anecdotal
prize of her AUTOGRAPHS book.

Gary Oldman, light of her life, fire of her loins. A stumbling of the tongue
in four steps to the coldest degree of nth on the roof of the mouth. Gare. Ree.
Old. Man.

Dear reader of hasty signatures, never speak syllables in the longitude of
obsession which can only be guessed at.

*

The AUTOGRAPHS book should be thrown out. Burned perhaps, I say to you, but only while you are sleeping with the windows open. Along with the smeared thumb-print in blood. Hers or possibly Gary Oldman's. I usually do not want to think like this before my errand into the wilderness, yet here we are because this is the metaphysical wilderness I am talking about.

You signed the postal slip yourself. You walked back up the stairwell to our apartment with it. You knew what the parcel contained and, once again, her well-traveled purse is here on our table, mailed with a return address. His address, in her writing. There, she says. That crummy neighborhood. An invite. A sign with no name. Meaning his. Another gentle man for me to find for your entertainment or edification or both.

Signatures, you have heard me contend on another night caretaking the same purse, are meant as evidence of chance encounters with people known and unknown who have left us forever, and the AUTOGRAPHS book an eternal sepulcher that even an award-winning actor like Gary Oldman himself will one day inhabit, though first in your famous sister's collection, populated with the beloved departed souls of famous American actors of the 1980's, such as Molly Ringwald and Tom Hulce, who constitute a couple of the primary ringleaders of these catacombs which you have me visit deep underneath the city night like Virgil leading Dante, not certain of what we will find but each antechamber filling itself with the foreboding of unwelcome anecdotes to come until our feet touch the ice. This is why every signature is always accorded its own page, its renown unable to share the space with lesser autographs of not-so-famous actors who could only aspire to become the next Gary Oldman, or perhaps the next Sid Vicious, or perhaps someone's famous sister, or perhaps a bloody anonymous thumb-print. Such are the various costs of failed fame in this life.

When you and her were teenagers in your civil servant parents' upstate home, she watched carefully, intently, repeatedly the scene in *Sid and Nancy* where Sid Vicious walks through a plate-glass door, and she had said to you, I, like, so gotta get Gary Oldman's signature. An AUTOGRAPHS book she has kept for years in her purse is a study of the depths she herself could plumb if only she could have walked through a plate-glass door at the Gehry Museum if it existed and discover the auto-hypnotic signature of Gary Oldman as Sid Vicious walking through a plate-glass door while signing his would-be name directly into the consciousness of a failed American etiquette which never knows what to do with itself inside a building where gentle men and gentle women hold open the doors. She knew then the accidental self-induced violence was not really accidental or even anecdotal, that the path to celebrity in America had nothing to do with the Warholian fifteen minutes suspended in potentiality of our ever-commoditized existence but a finger in the air, hovering, flailing to trace its path for the viewer looking on in horror or disbelief and find a name belonging to neither subject nor object, to neither Sid Vicious nor Gary Oldman, but to those who could never simply just walk through a building for no reason.

Like you and you all, for instance.

To walk through a building, I must open the door myself because, in the aberrant, self-loathing city, gentle men or gentle women are never entirely at my immediate disposal and because I do not mind opening doors for myself. I confess I enjoy opening my own doors, much in the same way those who have worked as dishwashers in restaurants find it soothing to wash the filthiest dishes by uncovered hand in their sink at home, even if they had used a machine at their previous job. It's true there is a certain unqualified shame in being forced to open my own doors in the city, but what do I care—I am neither famous nor particularly anecdotal. I am sensible and sense-ridden, however, which is why I take the elevator if it is working instead of walking up twelve flights in a dimly lit stairwell scaling upwards in a logical, orderly box which further unwinds as I ascend. I am frugal because it keeps occurring to me on the way up that I may never meet face-to-face the gentle man connected to your famous sister if I happen to unfortunately cross paths with someone doing a poor job of being Sid Vicious, unlike Gary Oldman who is always Sid Vicious in his movies and does a very good job at it, regardless of whether he is also a psychopathic murderous DEA agent or an unhappy Transylvanian prince or a self-mutilated sexual deviant or a Russian ne'er-do-well.

You and you all will be very disappointed to find out that I do not cross paths with any of these colorful roles in the hallway.

I cross paths with no one in the hallway. I only encounter the usual cacophony of thin voices wandering. Some are human, some televisional, some radiological, and some I wonder if they are an amalgam of things I could not possibly imagine happening behind all those closed doors and narrate to you, even though, you have told me, I have a very good imagination and am skilled at using it when it best suits me. I believe imagination is a terribly overrated thing and does too much work for us, like a gentle man or gentle woman who holds the door open for me though I derive pleasure from my own door-opening, especially if it is a plate-glass door I can completely see though. I am not so fortunate here in this apartment building because of the usual etiquette of privacy we expect in all buildings. Were I to stop at one of these opaque wooden doors thinking your famous sister may be behind one of them and put my hand to it try to imagine what those voices were alluding to or signifying, I would run the risk of having someone come out into the hallway—maybe even your famous sister—and find me silently placing my hand to the door as would a lonely pervert ready to let Jesus into his heart again, my only best colorful role here for you and you all, but not like Gary Oldman as Sid Vicious as a violent alcoholic, unconcerned about any and all doors and being chanced upon by an accidental audience.

No one ever steps into a hallway. Hallways are a vast corridor for the sake of being a vast corridor, designed specifically for intimidation and the false prospect of anecdotal behavior, channeling, separating, dividing and ensconcing us into our thin televisional and radiological voices meant to be heard by only gentle men and gentle women who have no company this evening.

The door I believe your famous sister is behind features the televisional voices I recognize from *Sid and Nancy* but not the voice of the gentle man she is watching it with. He is quiet, relaxed, somewhat perturbed, maybe uninspired, but still watching the movie with your famous sister all the same. He has been watching it over and over for days, weeks on end, giving particular attention at her behest to the scene where Gary Oldman as Sid Vicious walks through a plate-glass door. This happens, as the movie posits, because someone thoughtlessly distracts Sid Vicious at the crucial moment of proper entry into a building by calling out his name: execute the correct maneuver of etiquette by self-negation, or else suffer the consequences. Often I consider if one could internalize this distraction, whether doors as we know them could become obsolete or, in my more colorful dreams, we could eliminate the need for buildings altogether and reside in a world of mental architecture that does not punish us as an author who knows buildings well like Maurice Blanchot would have planned for us had he visited Niagara Falls or stayed at the Hotel Chelsea for no particular reason, not even for their fame. But all this imagination is asking too much of this particular gentle man who believes slowly, surely, and perhaps anecdotally that he has met the real Nancy Spungen, played by your famous sister, who he has been living with for days, weeks on end, maybe even months if he could recall. With my hand on the door I want to shout through it to him (assuming he has accepted our lord Jesus Christ as his personal savior) that your famous sister, while starring in many colorful roles, has never played Nancy Spungen nor has yet to completely walk through a plate-glass door like Sid Vicious or Gary Oldman playing Sid Vicious. On the other hand, she does have a good anecdote about meeting Gary Oldman at the Gehry Museum in Los Angeles if it existed, as she supports by taking out her AUTOGRAPHS book from her purse and flips to the single page with Gary Oldman's signature on it, including the bloody thumb-print.

You and I would expect that this is where your famous sister, under her own duress, begins a long reminiscing about her Gary Oldman encounter. The usual details surface: his generous yet unassuming physical attributes, the melodious amber-like quality of his voice which, over Time, has become more and more gentle and Americanized and not of a violent alcoholic household in London where he grew up, and how he calmly instructed her to stop the bleeding by applying firm yet gentle pressure with the makeshift tourniquet he fashioned out of an expensive Italian silk kerchief and applied to her hand—an unexpected gesture made more incomprehensible to you by your famous sister finding the AUTOGRAPHS book in her purse with her one good hand and having Gary Oldman sign it before the hairless person who was likely his agent pushed him along before the ambulance arrived, but not before the security arrived. The gentle man listens to this explanation carefully, jealously, but not acquiescingly, holding your famous sister's damaged hand and looking at the signature of a Gary Oldman he never fully understood and appreciated until now, until Gary Oldman as Sid Vicious. The Gary Oldman he only knew before as an incorruptible police lieutenant who later becomes a noble commissioner in an aberrant, self-loathing city would always have been a gentle man such as himself. He does not find this reverse paradigm shift an altogether disturbing prospect.

So Gary Oldman is your ur-friend, the gentle man finally says after a much dramatic pause as *Sid and Nancy* comes to its complete upteenth conclusion with Sid Vicious and Nancy Spungen cozying up in the afterlife reunion.

Your famous sister smiles. She is very pleased with this observation and agrees quickly, perhaps not too quickly, but quickly enough all the same so he will understand he has pleased her in an unexpected, fulfilling way which successful couples are known to reciprocate with each other in an exorbitant cohabitation scheme, something that neither he nor your famous sister are accustomed to. He secretly thanks the signature of Gary Oldman for this breakthrough though, all the while, the bloody thumb-print makes his skin itch. No longer is their relationship solely dictated by *Sid and Nancy* but by the kinship of Gary Oldman as sidewalk humanitarian and philanthropist which the gentle man can now recognize as though he were one who puts his hand on the door of an apartment belonging to whom he knows not in a building he never wanted to enter. Soon, very soon, his feet touch the ice along with your famous sister's in the last darkness he may know, walking, speaking in the anecdotes of one who must entertain his lover, continually tell his lover interesting stories, or risk losing that lover in a twelve-story building with no rooftop access but many doors to exit from. Your famous sister lets go of the gentle man's hand so she may reclaim the AUTOGRAPHS book from him. She has chosen these doors before with many prospective ur-friends in Los Angeles before her discharge, but not the anecdotal Gary Oldman who saved her from bleeding to death in front of the Gehry Museum if it existed outside of Gary Oldman's mind before security arrived—a true ur-friend indeed.

If only she had his phone number. Just to thank him again, of course.

Since I am neither assertive nor particularly noble, I cannot walk through the door or consider walking through the door or even imagine what lies beyond the door when the gentle man and your famous sister stop talking, when the thin voices all cease. Since I am reasonable and self-reasoned, I know when to remove my hand from the door, when to leave the hallway, and when to walk out of a building once I have no further reason to be there. Since I am all these things and possibly more, I do not enjoy being alone when I have no particular reason to be alone while the gentle man and your famous sister are not alone and possibly more in all things.

I return to our apartment with a greasy take-out pizza which we both eat quietly, passively, but not humbly with the windows open, the summer night, the sirens. You are not pleased with me yet. I have no anecdotes for you involving colorful roles encountered on the way back. Your famous sister is not here eating with us.

I appreciate how you always kept an eye on her, I imagine you may tell me much later in our own afterlife reunion which, sadly, resembles Virgil and Dante more than *Sid and Nancy* insofar as we will not touch each other until the explanations are all exhausted, the sinners punished, the ne'er-do-wells languishing in purgatory, and the virtuous rewarded for their gentle works. Which circle of the incorporeal comedy we will find your famous sister in all this, I try telling you before we abandon all hope, I really do not know. There are no circles in the afterlife reunion, says Gary Oldman, only a place where Sid Vicious eats his greasy pizza alone, waiting for Nancy Spungen to arrive unharmed. I speculate your famous sister will keep herself in this one building a little while longer with the gentle man who now sees *Sid and Nancy* as a cultural and philosophical touchstone as she understands it. Certain movies give us false hope like that. Yet this false hope is the last darkness you and I now move through with the thin televisional voices silenced, the radiological murmurings hushed, and the conversation of countless anecdotes about your famous sister, about the gentle man, even about Gary Oldman are brought to an abrupt and worthy end we would expect of successful couples who are known to reciprocate with each other, such as Sid Vicious and Nancy Spungen in the afterlife reunion of *Sid and Nancy*. They forgive each other, knowing there are people such as Gary Oldman and your famous sister who illuminate the message of their own lives so that we may put our hand on the door and feel their voices which will never belong to us, I want to tell you, holding you with more than hands, but desiring telling your famous sister instead.

Something not in the equality but of the pure, the enjoyment, you of name Nancy.

A blindness could be in the thin voices I press my hand to, in you in being her.

You do not see the Sid Vicious who walks through the plate-glass door but through the Gary Oldman the gentle man wishes would sign what his name is if I could draw my hand from the door your famous sister stands behind, waiting for me, I see, wanting nothing, no voices.

There are yet voices your sister would make famous for America, one by one, one in the stairwell, walking past twelve floors to the rooftop, one in the afterlife reunion, one on the sidewalk, not walking, and bleeding, all blood and signature but a thin voice getting less thin.

On the page that follows Gary Oldman.

The gentle man who thinks your sister is Nancy Spungen and he himself is Sid Vicious as Sid Vicious was who deserved not to walk up twelve flights of stairs but to die instead as Gary Oldman does not die but as Nancy Spungen must because she is not a gentle woman who has doors held open for her but is pushed off a rooftop of a building she was never supposed to enter because Sid Vicious either murders her or does not murder her at the Hotel Chelsea, according to Gary Oldman as Sid Vicious, with a knife never found in the afterlife reunion of her abdomen reduced to the thinning fame of a movie watched over and over and less and less and never again as the worn-down videotape then snaps, every scene and line of dialogue etched in the memory of the gentle man who once knew the gentle woman who played Nancy Spungen and knew all the famous actors of her day in her sleep where she found the knife and certain fame walking through the plate-glass door with the gentle man who is no longer a gentle man.

You and I stare at the signature of the gentle man as Sid Vicious who believes he is Gary Oldman as Sid Vicious after he kills Nancy Spungen. You stare at the signature longer than me, holding my hand, scanning over every word in the letter carefully, continuously, but not comprehendingly. I have already deciphered this letter's general significance despite it not being addressed to me but to you instead, despite that letter-writing, it is said, is something of a lost or dying art, despite that letters do not bring gentle news anymore but violent alcoholic tidings from that last darkness he will know regarding what has happened to your famous sister. The voluminous tears which are yours streak down the page, taking some of the ink with it, dropping with a pit-pit on your jeans though with you unaware of it and, watching the pit-pit on your leg start and swell and grow with each separate pit falling off the page until you become aware of it, I harmlessly swipe the stain, only making it worse.

Sid Vicious may have never cried once in his life with the possible exception of leaving his mother's womb (I have my own doubts). If *Sid and Nancy* can be believed, on the other hand, Nancy Spungen cried often and with intensity far into adulthood, never knowing a gentle man in her life but violent alcoholic types not far removed from Gary Oldman, regardless of their profession, awards won, or their propensity for walking through plate-glass doors. Sid Vicious may also have never written a letter in his life—not that I or any gentle person would have expected him to write one. Gary Oldman as Sid Vicious may have gone much longer without writing a letter so he could fully prepare for his role and capture the violent alcoholic style of Sid Vicious, imagining a gentle man who is not and never was a gentle man write and write and write and not write a single word of use or poetry or coherence but a letter continuing on and on about how Nancy Spungen died and that he did not mean to do it but really sort of did but just kind of, like, lost control of it all and himself and all he wanted was a gentle woman to take care of him but instead he got Nancy Spungen or someone he thought was Nancy Spungen who would not throw him off the roof of a building or follow him through the plate-glass door or listen to his blood go pit-pit on the floor of a building he never wanted to enter without Nancy Spungen in his afterlife reunion, do you bloody well get that, fucking signed, Sid.

You and I touch the letter. The signature which closely resembles Gary Oldman's in the AUTOGRAPHS book. The bloody well thumb-print beside it which remains anonymous.

I wonder why. Why is my imagination not rougher, more vulgar than this Sid Vicious who is now the gentle man your famous sister knew finally, lastly, but not gently, and who is writing from a building he may never leave except for the afterlife reunion with your famous sister who bears a passing resemblance to Nancy Spungen. If you forgive this gentle man who believes he is Sid Vicious, then I may forgive Gary Oldman for believing his violent alcoholic acting style would create every Sid Vicious known before there was such a person called Sid Vicious.

I want to tell you this and more, to explain it all away while you and I sit on our sofa in our apartment in the aberrant, self-loathing city. Yet I don't. You are trying to clean the watery ink from your jeans with your hand compulsively, obsessively, but not successfully. I take this unsuccessful hand of yours to make you stop, if only briefly, so you may hear the thin voices outside gathering in the longest of hallways you and I will travel down together, and hear him speak whom he believes your famous sister is.

STEPPIN OUT

IN THE DAYS AND WEEKS and months which you miss the company of your famous sister, you ask me again and again to go out and look for her or what is left of her or what has become of her or what has not become of her, like the days before and during when she was living with the gentle man who is no longer a gentle man, and, a bit more stunned than usual, I try to explain to you

(1) there was someone once in Los Angeles who was your famous sister, who bore a passing resemblance to Chloe Webb from *Sid and Nancy*, and then she met another person. It is peculiar how sometimes meeting another person—another person who is not your doppelganger—can be equated to death itself, or at least resemble death in some way, but the occasional disappearance of our corporeal self into a building with this gentle person who we choose to spend all our days with cannot be denied when I mull over how long it has been since I have heard from your upstate civil servant parents since I met you on this very same sofa years ago and how this sofa has become, in every sense of the word, the bedrock of our exorbitant cohabitation scheme and I can only every think of returning to you each and every day on this sofa where we now discuss your famous sister at such length that it is almost like she lives with us as we had originally intended, which is the tack I try taking with you, the old

41

hand, She hasn't really left us, She'll always be with us if—and thus I start my long trail of reminisces which are not successful reminisces because

(2) I have very little conception of what she actually did in Los Angeles, other than putting her arm through a plate-glass door at the Gehry Museum if it existed; and this is the moment impressed upon me to celebrate with you every night, doing what we can to forget Gary Oldman and the unfortunate grip he wielded over your famous sister—you're sure he didn't mean it, he never meant it, though, supposing, if, however, he, did, meaning, however, really, it, could, however, be, unless, somehow, he, if, he spends his days in waiting for your famous sister to return when he is done shooting a scene for the day with his hairless agent pours himself a double bourbon in a hand-etched highball glass leather chair big comfy fire going in his studio he sits and things of that crazy American woman who thought for sure that he was Gary Oldman even if at that moment he was trying to be anyone but Gary Oldman, a passive observer trying to take in the Gehry Museum if it existed and see a special multi-room video installation by a famous Korean artist he had heard so much about, and the fame of that artist spread over him like the warmth of good Kentucky bluegrass in an amber liquid and gave him joy when he first took sight of the Gehry Museum's magnificence if that also existed and he knew then

(3) the presence of what he desired took the form of a building, and that building was the most splendid, ethereal thing he had ever witnessed in his life since every building he had ever walked through or inhabited since he can remember was a place where all desires die, where his own desires were slowly, surely, but not carefully snuffed out and substituted for the desires of another until the need to act, to put form to formlessness in the wreck of his body, overwhelmed him and allowed him to subsume all that was necessary to have a life including Sid Vicious; then your famous sister comes along on the sidewalk, or, that is, she straggles alongside herself with arm dangling bleeding barely working enough to pull a pen and cheap AUTOGRAPHS book out of her purse which she asks to him sign, if he'd please, she was a huge fan of his work—he noted that, always his work, never a fan of him—and despite the protests of his hairless agent he signed the book taking care not to get any blood on himself, which he did

anyways but having to leave the Gehry Museum outside with ambulance and security and arriving, too many people paying attention, and her, her right in front of him, whom he would know later, much later, that *her*, and that he would hate her forever

(4) knowing the Gehry Museum, if it were to exist for him because supposedly he never entered it because of your famous sister, is an aberrant, self-loathing city unto itself filled with the collective auspices of gentle men and gentle women who are not famous who give themselves over to gentle culture which wishes not to be gentle and yet here it is, in a building of ten thousand mirrors showing ten thousand raised eyebrows hovering over a single painting done by a single gentle person, not at all recognizing the collective properties of any given work of culture, such as the work of Gary Oldman, an actor of significant cultural import who has been many things unto all and all things unto himself and it is only other gentle people who bring him into existence, like this building, and those who are not gentle cannot see or enter the building because the building does not exist while they refuse to recognize the omnipresence of Gary Oldman reaching out to sign Los Angeles in the blood of your famous sister while he waits for security to arrive, wondering if he will ever get to see the world famous Gehry Museum, but not now, not now that all the gentle people inside know that he, Gary Oldman, is outside, tending to a gentle woman who is no longer gentle with his hairless agent tugging at his arm to leave the premises immediately before there is a scene

and (5) the Gary Oldman who often wishes that he listen to his hairless agent less and less but since Gary Oldman is an agent of nothing in particular other than all things unto himself, he unfortunately has to listen to him, remembering the unfortunate circumstances he learned from *Sid and Nancy* of what happens when Nancy Spungen is allowed to be the agent of Sid Vicious, looking upon this poor bleeding woman in a new light like the second coming of Chloe Webb, leaving himself fixed to the spot, his hairless agent's pleas falling on deaf ears, Gary, Gary, c'mon let's go, let's leave,

yet Gary Oldman doesn't listen as you don't listen, stubbornly, consistently, but not vacuously. Your famous sister and her immutable soul are easy enough to let go. Only the whereabouts of her are causing all the significant narrative problems.

The building where the gentle man who is no longer a gentle man now resides looks nothing like the Gehry Museum if it existed, nor Mann's Chinese Theater, to be sure, nor even the Hotel Chelsea if it were designed by Maurice Blanchot. It most certainly does not look like Niagara Falls if Niagara Falls were a building. You and I enter it all the same, closely, carefully, but not anonymously by the gentle request of those people who work in this building who would rather not work in it—at least judging by their close, careful anonymity.

You and I are used to entering buildings such as this one before your famous sister was discharged in Los Angeles. You may not be as used to it as I am, I who know very well the hallways of thin voices who resemble Gary Oldman in his various colorful roles and sometimes even a role I do not recognize, which can be disconcerting if you are someone who must walk these hallways, is paid or impelled to do so. At least I have experience on my side and the invisible truncheon of authority as I narrate my own way down the hallway and place my hand on the door so that I may imagine a gentle man who is no longer a gentle man speak his thin televisional or radiological voice into an architecture where etiquette does not exist but in the bearer of experience who may show the other person—such as you—how it is done.

Sometimes I wonder, as I push a strand of your hair behind your ear, if you resent me for my experience, how this experience ruins the surprise for you of what happens when the door opens and you see the subject inside and the subject inside is not any different that the subject outside. You ask yourself why you did not recognize the subject outside like you wonder why more people do not recognize your famous sister. The answer, it seems to me, is we do not want to recognize the subject outside. The subject outside can never possibly be outside, which is why, when we see them, we can barely believe our eyes and want to say in our confusion, It can't possibly be him or her or it. Strange longing for a gender determinant aside, it is almost as if it is a terrible disappointment emerges seeing the subject outside the door, to be forced to consider the subject beyond televisional and radiological voices growing less and less thin. We wish this would stay behind the door forever, such as the gentle man who is no longer a gentle man, though if the gentle man is Sid Vicious, then there is no door he can stay behind, no plate-glass door he cannot walk through, no building that can keep him while he waits for Nancy Spungen in the afterlife reunion, eating a greasy slice of pizza which, as Gary Oldman reminds us of in *Sid and Nancy*, is his favorite food without hesitation.

The gentle man who is no longer a gentle man is not exactly Sid Vicious in this particular building, if only because he still resides in it and will not be leaving it anytime soon. This is what the people in this particular building assure you and I calmly, professionally, but not convincingly. There will be other buildings the gentle man who is no longer a gentle man may yet reside in, with their own hallways, with their own opaque doors, with their own thin voices which mimic his and render him completely anonymous and not as Sid Vicious, which may constitute the worst form of punishment in this building, as it is the worst form of punishment in this life not to be Gary Oldman when he is being Gary Oldman, famous actor, standard-bearer for every Sid Vicious before anyone ever knew Sid Vicious would become the bassist for The Sex Pistols who could not really play the bass guitar.

Since Gary Oldman is a building the gentle man who is no longer a gentle man must now walk through, I tell you Gary Oldman can be neither British nor American but a nationality unto himself which resists tradition and convention such as those aforementioned countries. I admit nationalities do not concern me, only insofar as they project certain notable, intangible attributes of personality distinct to that geographical region of the world. Those attributes are carried across in televisional and radiological voices which we must put our hand to and feel their reverberations like the lonely perverts each one of us must become when watching television or listening to music. Nationality is only another perversion, then. We all may put our hands to these reverberations which best dictate how we say who we are, but the beauty of Gary Oldman has shown us that a violent alcoholic personality of deep yearning and frustration is a country of no boundaries, of no territories, but of many many perverts both lonely and notable, ready to stake their claim as they descend through building after building until they arrive at the Gehry Museum in Los Angeles which exists only in the mind of Gary Oldman and walk through the plate-glass door of an etiquette with no nationality, in a building with no gentle men or gentle women, and into the afterlife reunion. For matters of convenience, however, you and I are forced to identify ourselves because you and I have the freedom to be forced to do so. If, for instance, I were to claim my nationality to the people in this building as *Sid Vicious*, my lonely perversion would become far too obvious and metaphorically scream from a rooftop where I may later fall off of in a drunken stupor, because, in America, in this building, no one can be a lonely pervert when he or she says, I am an American, much in the same way Gary Oldman cannot be a lonely pervert when he says, I am British. You and I know he is as much British as he is American and, despite that he has played being an American very well, Jesus has yet to enter his heart as you and I have entered this building whose only purpose is that we must leave it with the sense of ourselves intact while discussing the whereabouts of what remains of your famous sister.

I think, but do not tell you, the gentle man who is no longer a gentle man wants to destroy your beauty in this building. He wants you to see overworked people in buildings, hunched over, looking at their own little private glowing buildings, ignoring their own unhappy children who cannot enter these buildings yet but will someday. He wants you to sit and keep waiting in this building.

While we sit and wait and keep waiting in the building which is required in all buildings such as this one because walking through it when you do not belong to it is strictly prohibited they tell us through sign and signature, you take out the latest personal technology with tiny earphones from your purse and soon begin humming the entire playlist to The Sex Pistol's *Never Mind the Bollocks, Here's the Sex Pistols*, which, as you have told me and as I understood before putting my hand on our bedroom door listening to Johnny Rotten's uncorrupted radiological voice of sneer and disdain for all forms of etiquette, is one of your favorite albums—along with the soundtracks to *Pretty in Pink* and *Amadeus*, strangely or not strangely enough. This album had significant cultural import to you and your famous sister growing up in your civil servant parents' upstate home, but only after you watched *Sid and Nancy* and then, with great interest, Gary Oldman as Sid Vicious walking through a plate-glass door and you were, like, I so gotta listen to The Sex Pistols, which you did constantly, repeatedly, but not passively during the 1980's in an America which required a passive tolerance of all forms of etiquette. You and your famous sister refused to open doors for anyone, particularly gentle men, because that was something only your civil servant parents would do when entering buildings upstate. But *Sid and Nancy* had set you both free of that notion. Your humming *Never Mind the Bollocks* now seems to me a seething, self-loathing gesture as we sit in this building, a building for which I held open the door for you as we entered. I know you prefer not having doors opened for you, but I am trying to be gentle myself in light of what has happened between your famous sister and this gentle man who is no longer a gentle man, thus avoid reminding you that, musically speaking, Sid Vicious contributed very little or nothing to *Never Mind the Bollocks.*

I see regardless, with you nodding away to your latest personal technology, you can be beautiful in any building not in the Los Angeles of Gary Oldman's mind, providing it is a beauty which requires a careful suspension of traditional and popular notions of beauty that the work of Gary Oldman has helped the world understand, a suspension of the thin voices often interfering with gentle men and gentle women recognizing true beauty, which is why they need Gary Oldman's acting and its violent alcoholic intensity. They need to realize, as you do, that, like, Sid Vicious was once a beautiful man corrupted by the influence of etiquette in his life, which you see and recognize in that you are something of a beautiful man yourself when you, too, are suspended in the laughter bursting from a building where no laughter is usually found because what is usually found is the gentle man who is no longer a gentle man but not exactly Sid Vicious, either, despite what he has done. Yet because of Gary Oldman you realize even Sid Vicious cannot exactly be Sid Vicious anymore. He cannot be the bassist of The Sex Pistols who really did not know how to play bass but knew how to be the best violent alcoholic he could so someone like a future Gary Oldman could find him beautiful in his own suspension of traditional and popular notions of beauty which could not be contained in any building, even in the Gehry Museum in Los Angeles if it existed. It is the beauty of Gary Oldman as Sid Vicious, then, which also walks through the plate-glass door with the deliberate intention of accident, undenied, and uncorrupted by the American etiquette you and your famous sister rebelled against while upstate and recognized the plate-glass door you and her would someday have to walk through yourselves if you ever come to know this beauty of Sid Vicious which

Gary Oldman is the sole arbiter of so you may find your own afterlife reunion with Sid Vicious as gentle man eating pizza alone until you arrive, whether or not I may be there, the least beautiful person in your life because I am with you now, here, in this building, saying nothing much.

Your famous sister is not unknown to the people in this building, though their familiarity with the work of a certain Gary Oldman is far greater than hers, though the gentle man who is no longer a gentle man has assisted them in that regard, though *Sid and Nancy* is not considered a great movie of significant cultural import among the people who work in this building, though the idea of an afterlife reunion is tenuous at best for them. The fame your famous sister derives here is not from any AUTOGRAPHS book but of a muted, pewter quality which only reluctantly shines when even the strongest light is shone upon it, as if to say, I am only pewter because you shine this crude light on me in this building where the pretense of etiquette exists.

You and I answer their bore-reen questions about your famous sister with patience, exactitude, but not ebullience, feeling the crudeness of their light in this building designed by no one with a myriad of narrow windows and florescent lights and opaque doors reverberating with thin voices neither of the televisional or radiological variety but of a different quality even I am not accustomed to sensing or imagining. Sensing or imagining this yourself, you sit with cold anticipation in our chairs while you and I wait for our feet to touch the ice so they may no longer touch the ice anymore but release us into a world without bore-reen questions which, unfortunately, is the world without your famous sister, condemned by the people in this building because they must ask about her in the interrogative form where nothing is ever complete or known or entirely satisfactory to their narrative, or fitting into a pre-conceived narrative anticipating their satisfaction. And so, in a Time like this, it is comforting to talk about Gary Oldman's latest role now playing in theaters, which requires no questions at all, only a belief in an afterlife reunion where there are no buildings but only Sid Vicious and Nancy Spungen forgiving each other over a slice of pizza as if they will be a gentle man and a gentle woman unto each other into eternity, driving off in a driverless taxi cab with jubilant dancing black boys running after them.

Then you are bold. During the questions you ask for something as Gary Oldman would ask for something. Something I expected and dreaded yet am thrilled about.

You ask the people in the building for a copy of the letter the gentle man who is no longer a gentle man sent you (and, in effect, me as well, though I hardly have occupied his thoughts up until now, especially as a narrator). The people in the building are unsure of this request. The letter is evidence, after all, a virtual admission of guilt, and they would not want anything to disrupt the proceedings of legal etiquette against him with the people in another building. When those proceedings are over, they may grant you a photocopy. You are not satisfied with this compromise. You demand firmly, assuredly, but not politely that you require a perfect facsimile of the original letter, including the same shade of red of the bloody anonymous thumb-print in its original unsaturated hue, suitable for framing. The people in the building are uncertain of this request, telling you they may be unable to grant it, also suggesting you may never see this letter again as it is, as how the gentle man intended it to be seen, as how the signature would one day rival the importance of Gary Oldman's signature, or at least harbor as much mystery and sophistication as his. For now that is an impossibility, at least within this building. In another building, the signature of a gentle man who is no longer a gentle man may carry substantial legal weight and psychological intrigue and cultural status one of these days, as it will forever be connected to your famous sister, and everyone who knows the famous American actors of the 1980's will almost assuredly know her as well. Perhaps even those famous actors themselves.

The people in this building will not let us speak directly with the gentle man who is no longer a gentle man, but they thank us again for passing along the letter with the bloody thumb-print, which they have analyzed behind an opaque door somewhere over there where you and I cannot see.

In the meantime, your direct relation to your famous sister is of little consequence to the people in this building, and they leave you hoping for better buildings to come, bigger buildings holding more beautiful and enlightened people than this one. Then you catch yourself before this thought corrupts you any further. You know those beautiful, enlightened people have never existed— except, that is, in buildings like the Gehry Museum in Los Angeles.

The days and weeks and months without your famous sister to worry about and tend to are an unwelcome adjustment, days and weeks and months in which you no longer have to worry about her and tend to her in the conventional or contrived sense, or put out flyers that will be torn down by disinterested parties or Jesus-free perverts or other roaming ne'er-do-wells with only the faintest intellectual capacity to recognize how Gary Oldman permeates the human condition, or start researching facilities that could have helped her avoid visiting the concrete handprints at Mann's Chinese Theater. In some way, long after receiving the gentle man who is no longer a gentle man's letter, it is something of a relief all the same, prompting you to contend sisterhood is no burden. You are uncertain as to what to say to your civil servant parents upstate who have not corresponded to you about what has happened to their least favorite daughter. It would not be the first occasion.

I suppose I'm alone, you say forlornly, wistfully, but not proudly. You mull over this cruel development of having only myself and the black boy you socially counsel at the social building as your company hereafter, continually crossing the levels, entering and leaving buildings with no particular relevance to our lives, structure imparting form, form imparting shape, shape imparting purpose, at last. But what purpose is there when we have no more buildings to enter observing the proper etiquette, when only the example of your famous sister walking through a plate-glass door is the model for the remainder of your bore-reen life.

To alleviate this discrepancy, you decide to watch movies with me on the sofa. It is very easy to do so with my penchant for cinematic guidance. Many many movies to select from thanks to the latest technology, too. Mostly from Ingmar Bergman, Stanley Kubrick, Akira Kurosawa, Alfred Hitchcock, David Lean, and Abbas Kiarostami as primary examples I show, a limitless world of beautiful, enlightened mental architecture at your disposal where Gary Oldman in any incarnation does not roam, which also means your famous sister does not roam there as well. She is safely ensconced somewhere in private memory where you and I will not cross paths with her, or at least not watch her play a game of chess with Death itself, even if the residuum of her least favorite pastime gently knocks at our door and asks us from the laundry room in the basement to consider replacing Max Van Sydow in the match, then reconsider her company for the evening since we do not plan on commiserating with our ur-friends, anyway, much less our few actual friends remaining.

You and I cannot watch movies forever, however, much like how America cannot make movies forever until these populate the afterlife reunion for Sid

Vicious and Nancy Spungen to watch when they get bored of talking to each other constantly.

So you and I are wont to step out, as is said, one step following the next.

And step away we do. Away from all the doors. Away from all the buildings.

When you and I step out and do what Gary Oldman cannot, which is to wander in public and observe our fellow humans in their quasi-natural state while we ourselves are observed, we thus reenact the enduring ritual of existence to expose ourselves to every little thing at the risk of our lives, or at least our sanity, our convictions. Not even the gentle man who is no longer a gentle man will be afforded this simple luxury again because he has willingly relinquished it, which haunts our thoughts—an existing building one *deliberately* chooses to never leave, the horror—as we circle the paths into a neat, manicured Japanese garden and feel the necessary relief of tranquility, order, the sense of intuition being fed which must please our appetites like a seasoned *flâneur*. You and I are better for all this, surrounded by only gentle men and gentle women who appreciate the same and harbor no ill memories of Sid Vicious or even Gary Oldman as Sid Vicious since *Sid and Nancy* is not a movie of great cultural import, since Alex Cox is not Bergman, not Kubrick, not even Tobe Hooper. No no no. There are only gentle people here like those visiting the grand temples of Kyōtō, and they find the centuries-old gardens to their satisfaction, the patterns in the very fine sand weaving and crossing over each other, forming those indistinct islands our minds inhabit, contemplating in the most shame-inducing secrecy why these rocks are infinitely more fascinating than other gentle people, especially when they lack the ability to step out.

Yet it is while walking aimlessly among these rocks you realize there is nothing more to our gainful employment in the aberrant, self-loathing city. You and I are, in fact, now employed by the gentle man who is no longer a gentle man, the sole reason being for him to stay in the building, to be tended to by other people, so we may provide him all the essential services he requires to conduct himself in his cell. I have been playing no small part here thus far to attempt recording all potentialities of his experience and existence and provide all means of listening to the gentle man who last knew your famous sister and granted his audience her own experience which neither you nor your upstate civil servant parents could convey, not while you all are employed by the story of your famous sister the familial memory gives us, sentimental, unsentimental, skewed, accurate, it matters little. It remains another narrative bought and sold in a building somewhere upstate where clueless neighbors come to inquire about children, where the gentle people in this building knock on doors at other buildings to ask about the whereabouts of so-and-so when they already know where, where relatives never dare to tread for fear of the impropriety of voiding station—their own in particular—and hence rely on other channels if not pure imagination. Those other channels are already there and willing. All the televisional and radiological voices which give them and us exactly the information they need regarding your famous sister, filling in the gaps of knowledge, confirming basest fears. They want to make us so very happy

gentle men who are no longer gentle men exposing her whole façade for what it was, shining bright light on that unknowable pewter of a famous sister of yours who, condolences aside in your Time of need, clearly was no better than anyone else but much worse than they thought,

all these rocks sing to you and me in the garden of earthly delights.

AS A SOCIAL WORKER,
WITH YOUR KEATSIAN FLAIR

WHEN WATCHING YOU in the morning before you leave for your social building, taking in your banal habit of private ritual, I do so with rare insight of your attention fixated on something resembling the intransient. Like, both your famous sister and the gentle man who is no longer a gentle man. With these two people not entirely removed from your thoughts yet, every little thing requires a focus of such intensity so you may draw a hot bath in the same manner you and her drew a hot bath when you were living upstate with your civil servant parents, letting most of the early water pass into the drain until the later water reaches the optimal temperature, which, in this building, can take anywhere from seven to twelve minutes—a lifetime for an experienced narrator such as myself to observe you sitting on the toilet, seat down, your underfed legs crossed, with your chin in your hand in pensive contemplation of the steam rising just enough from the white claw-footed porcelain to suggest all appearances are beautiful presumptive of a motionless quality which is not actually true before I have had my coffee.

Often I do believe this is the most beautiful way I or anyone else inclined to anecdotal behavior could ever see a gentle person prior to helping people who are not altogether gentle. *Natural expression*, it has been called by better narrators. It is something of a privilege I indulge without belying my lack of interest. I do not have to say anything whatsoever but let you sit there as I shave with the latest shaving technology and unsuccessfully slick-down my permanent morning cowlick, all the while calculating the best moment to tell you Los Angeles has not called me yet, my services have not been picked up for the commercial which will advertise the latest personal technology—whatever it may be—and that we are behind on rent and owe some money elsewhere, in another building. All because you have had me spend too much Time looking for your famous sister in too many hallways in too many buildings when I should have been narrating something else, then remembering you, too, have not been working much as of late.

Perhaps this is what you are thinking about if not my vague, futile acts of combined physical and mental hygiene.

But the steam grows hotter as you continue to sit there longer, the mirror steaming up faster than its slowness suggests until I can no longer discern whether I am making any progress on my permanent morning cowlick. Drawing my hand across the mirror leaves in the cleared trail a reflection—you moving up behind me. You throw your arms underneath mine in a maneuver not unlike what gentle people who pretend not to be gentle call a *full nelson* tossing me to the side of the white claw-footed porcelain trying hurling my head into water scalding me peel burn skin off even with my hands at other side of the tub preventing this curse on your lips you learned from the black boy at the social building to direct me into scalding water, to punish, to teach, I don't know.

I'm scared you may do this. You may succeed for once. Your success has been predicated upon me knowing your susceptibility to those brief moments of fury which punctuate the violent alcoholic works of Gary Oldman.

This is what you've done before with your sister, you had explained to me, panting, exhausting us on the bathroom floor, this testing the water's heat with your own reluctant hand, forced in there by your famous sister who could do this to you without any fear of reproach or your civil servant parents listening, downstairs, watching television, watching the neighbors, and them letting the two of you make sure that you don't let the other drown before bedtime. No one could hear anything anyway, really, especially with the volume up on the *Pretty in Pink* or *Amadeus* cassette soundtrack playing on the stereo in your bedroom because this is, like, America in the 1980's I am talking about.

*

As a social worker in the aberrant, self-loathing city, you never claim to be as social or anecdotal as you should be with your clients, or, at least, it was easier to talk them up during the first year of your employment at the social building, before the black boy came along, when the profanity there was only dish-soap mild or sometimes steely-tinged but never completely out of hand, never an eternal curse. Having a famous sister helped prepare you for this employment, as well as prompted you trying it, already feeling too inured having helped your famous sister but perhaps treating many clients would allow you perspective, innocently understanding her obsessions and compulsions which gradually wore down your civil servant parents and their secret upstate disappointment over having children to begin with, leaving them to give up, hey, go do what you want, sure, doing little to hide this disappointment after trying so hard to hide your famous sister from the world. A fair chance they could recoup their losses with you someday. The loss of pride, the loss of name which you yourself dare not mutter to me for fear I will find something in it, if not meaning, is but an idea of you which I try to convey to our upstairs neighbor, having only her to explain my situation to, and her having only an old man with yellowish white hair look on while he sits patiently on her bed and nod and interpret the face of the one he desires. All these unfulfilling roles needing play. Seldom casting them off.

Everything you hold moves between hallways filled with all the faces of the lost who do not have a story redeemable, the same story told, the same story of other buildings you hear again and again in this social building. I have filled your imagination with all that can be told thanks to the narratively regenerative properties of Gary Oldman and his illustrious acting career, culminating in a chance encounter between your famous sister and him in Los Angeles in front of the Gehry Museum if it existed that we can never confirm happened as though it were an appendage sliced off, growing anew until fitting the host body perfectly, every instance of decompensation or backsliding or romantic entanglement leading to the face of he who ruined your famous sister seen in unwashed unstable eyes looking for the release of the audience, a very good audience who will not applaud but explain everything, give back what has been so generously received with pain and exactitude, you pulling, slicking down your frizzy hair into a tight ponytail so you don't have to do anything more with it, looking for your clients in the lame cubicle office you keep with six other social workers to acknowledge this irrefutable fact I keep trying to smother.

A sad fact remains: I can't remember your face when you leave me for the day. So I must remember your famous sister's instead.

This substitution, of course, can be easily accomplished because of her resemblance to Chloe Webb which, in turn, resembles Nancy Spungen which, in conclusion, resembles the face of every upstate prodigy-turned-failure I have ever crossed paths with in hallways, especially when factoring my Time spent with her watching *Sid and Nancy* over and over before she went to Los Angeles, which I had never watched before until meeting her, never taking in the narratively regenerative properties of Gary Oldman as Sid Vicious until witnessing each afterlife reunion move her softening face into the twitching anecdotal. In every driverless taxi cab speeding away there expired a signpost for what she herself thought she had experienced but was never entirely certain of until, like, Gary Oldman showed her authenticity in the form of a violent alcoholic acting style making her understand her end, and how it would happen, though it would not happen with me, she knew or she complained, because I had you to return to when I came back to my senses, when I realized who your famous sister really was, surrounded by ur-friends so she could move toward the only terminus her fame would allow so she could finally be released from it. Lucky her.

You have never asked any of your fellow social workers or the clients with their pants down to keep an eye out or an ear pressed on a door for your famous sister, even if they are familiar with *Sid and Nancy*, out of a sense of that upstate shame passed along like heredity—not that you have a sister, no, but because she is famous in a way that fame has now become, beyond understanding etiquette which accords such flawed privilege. Finding your famous sister is a priority, one that you have done over and over with these not-famous people who you see at this social building with their crumpled dirty hats and penitent hands in their laps. They are too ashamed to admit they are not famous and never will be, with the exception of the black boy with the eternal curse on his lips seeking a different fame, a client you admire and dread as though he were steam in a bathroom rising from white claw-footed porcelain, a penumbra you cannot fully comprehend yet despite the context of *Sid and Nancy* with Sid being serenaded facetiously by a throng of black boys as foreplay to the afterlife reunion with Nancy. You wonder if these clients— the black boy in particular—are serenading you as well, unaware of your connection to your famous sister or who you are beyond a social worker who requires this foreplay to return to me, your narrator, on the sofa at night to make sense of those who you have talked up or attempt to talk up while they squirm uncomfortably in the dirty plastic molded seat when you ask them, What's happened since we last talked

sometimes looking at them with those eyes you are not allowed to have in the social building because seeing a quality forbidden in this building when you are you, when you are with me witnessing what we do before our feet touch the ice below, before Gary Oldman pays us a visit in his latest incarnation which, unless Sid Vicious counts, he has never played, in this case, a client with a crumpled dirty hat and penitent hands in his lap whom you have never seen before, smiling and nodding to you, though you have never seen them before, though they act as though they have, and, in fact, they have seen you before, they have seen you everywhere because you have never seen them, the one role which Gary Oldman has never taken for himself—for clients have machinations, desires, perversions, secret enemies—but not these clients who sit near us anticipating our friendly reciprocity which, in a manner of speaking, is then returned to them without cautious gaze of inquiry and skepticism as you want to ask them by not asking,

What hallways have you walked down at night when everyone is asleep, whose heart did you hold in your patient hand and soothe it to rest of what is to come when you realize there are too many doors to tend, too many buildings to walk through alone

knowing the various gentle people in your life who you see in other buildings complain that I never spend much Time with you, or enough Time, or all the Time in the world—the latter a concept so fantastic to me I often forget myself on the sofa pondering its myriad interpretations, the world being old enough as it is to me at present, and this is how I regard you, as old enough for me, barely, given the arbitrary, unknowable line of oldness and its acceptability of me having your company while I feign hyperventilation just so you can pay me a little attention that I do not really need or want, so you can place your hand on my chest, knowing full well the symptoms of the actual ailment, but leave it there, neglecting to tell me, It's going to be all right, but telling me of your day and of your very special clients, the black boy who never becomes gentle around you, forever at odds with your social building and everyone in it as if he has all the Time in the world to be a black boy, which you may think he does, in a way, pressing my chest, holding my breathing at your pace of telling anecdotes about the black boy, a transient to the buildings of this aberrant, self-loathing city where everyone has their hurry down to a simple etiquette of, ExcusemebutIhavetogonowbye

you taking keys from the table and leaving me on the sofa, recovered enough to your own satisfaction of what my little theater provides as the antithesis of gainful employment through narration. This is why you like the black boy. It isn't because he doesn't have a job or enough food to eat, but the work and its etiquette lose its significance when you enter the building thinking your famous sister will suddenly appear and instead it is a black boy who curses at you, curses the other social workers employed by the building, curses any other people whom you have never heard of and probably he hasn't heard of, either, but a long, deliberate, cascading curse filling the hallways with such depths of profanity that it threatens to reach out and subsume all the gentle people who are no longer gentle in its expanding, aimless invective against the social building, including yourself, the difference being you don't feel the brunt of this curse, having been insulated by the gentle man who is no longer a gentle man and a letter signed with a bloody thumb-print and what has happened to your famous sister, to the point where you expect it, even ask of it from the black boy with his tears streaming, teeth bared, and the profanity that reaches into antiquity before there was ever gentleness and before anyone placed words at the feet of an audience desiring gentleness

that beauty is truth, truth beauty, and the beauty crude to the truth beauty when really one is moved by a truth for nothing beautiful fully true to you and your truth beauty that is moving you about me, really one less truthful, and hence of less beauty than truth beauty, loose to the touch of you less and less, or lesser still, not moving, not fully one for nothing beautiful, for you about me is about knowing, yet to know can be less than truthful to being moved by those less than you or me, who elude every touch in full view of others

knowing what truth beauty needs of you, really, still nothing yet to know but
beauty is truth being told by a moving you feel fully knows me, I who am far
less beautiful now that your truth lessens me to another's life all for nothing
if not the knowing itself of anything not true, anything that is not you but
really me, nothing to anything, others who more fully in full view can never be
another, never be less than truthful, for every touch in full view does not move
at all, knowing well their beauty is not full, all for nothing if not being moved
away so another may say, I who am far less truthful have yet to know you
about me, proving the truth beauty that beauty itself is when no truth stays
in your full view while moved by my thinking, which eludes these, known by
you, another in another life now known is all you need to know

    about the beauty of Gary Oldman as a client with a crumpled dirty hat
and penitent hands in his lap is that he is already there—which is to say, he
is here—thinking that you and I require his company, even if the truth is
far from it, that the last thing you and I want to see is Gary Oldman in any
incarnation, particularly this one, because we cannot stand to see him as a
gentle man who has always been a gentle man, even when he was a child in
a violent alcoholic household in London, the shame that you and you felt
remembering the Gary Oldman as Sid Vicious and how much you and you
all loved him for it and wished to marry yourselves to the ur-friend you could
never marry because there is no marriage except marrying yourselves to the
ur-friend who refuses it, who sits in the sun, drinking coffee, and waits for you
and I to arrive so someone may hear the anecdotes of an aberrant, self-loathing
city, if not you, if not you with me, if not you with me here, an impossibility, a
truth beauty untold for reasons I could give but never make you believe

    the beauty of a bloody thumb-print one can't account for as signature, that
our upstairs neighbor can't account for, not without taking the edge in one's
hand, paper or porcelain, and finding it when we speak of truth beauty and
beauty is without the face of another to ruin it in a memory, when we make
our way past all the others who have only those memories to return them to
the buildings they once roamed in the absence of true perpetuity, fearing the
truth beauty of perpetuity which they sought to avoid, having forever to avoid
a bloody anonymous thumb-print that belonged to a client once—and may
in fact belong to all of them if they subscribe to a particular fact-killing of
themselves—or it will belong to them someday, and soon, very soon, feeling
there is nothing they can really avoid without the helping hand of etiquette to

hold open the door for them when they enter, having survived this building on so many occasions thanks to gentle men and gentle women who wish them only the best, to stem the tide of every bloody anonymous thumb-print which may grace the edge of paper or porcelain for us to hold onto

but I know the I knows no beauty truth from beauty is, having known your famous sister, having known you, you both of twin occupation and obsession I cavort with when not wandering the hallways at night thinking of the bloody anonymous thumb-print signing my life to a letter having nothing to do with me but everything to do with you looking around, finding things to send to your civil servant parents upstate, looking for any trace of Gary Oldman to purge from your life, weary of occupation and obsession, weary of buildings, weary of fact-killing and having nothing but memory, now knowing it cannot be a truth beauty because the beauty has been forever corrupted like the aberrant, self-loathing city Gary Oldman forever roams and cannot be saved save for the act of walking through a plate-glass door and showing beauty is what truth truth beauty takes shape when the shape is ruined, walking into buildings we must walk through if we are ever to actually leave it when the building leaves us without what beauty is.

Often, while I try sleeping on the sofa alone during the evenings that you have tried to scald or drown me in the white claw-footed porcelain with hot water, it remains difficult not to think you are there with me on the sofa.

A morose projection of past and future simultaneous: the old habit, that oldest part of longing for the other. I know you are long gone but I keep you with me, not as memory but the sense of what it felt like lying next to you when you didn't try to kill me, the peaceful moments saved from endless occupation about your famous sister, where no gentle man who is no longer a gentle man could touch us with his influence, whether in the form of thin televisional voices or his letter affixed with a bloody anonymous thumb-print which may not be his but you and I know it is, the gentleness which we cannot escape because he cannot escape the building Gary Oldman has left him in for perpetuity, thinking the afterlife reunion lies ahead of him so he and your famous sister will one day spend all of one day together that lasts forever. I would tell them the only eternal can't only be lying alone on a sofa thinking of you not at all repentant for your attempted scalding of me because unless it happened it didn't really happen, meaning never, meaning never a potential.

When my imagination fails utterly, completely, but not predictably, I will show you the hallways I have roamed in lives not my own. I can never say whether I will make this happen for you when you enter the next building looking for your famous sister in the story of every client who walked in the shadow of another, in the lives and sighs spoken in resentment of etiquette that you are forever subject to, too afraid to leave the social building and enter armed with another story belonging to neither gentle man nor gentle woman, nor even a gentle child—if these exist in the social building—but the indiscriminate crush of bodies all pressed together at once, filling the building, overwhelming even the most seasoned social worker until their feet can no longer find and interpret the ice as something inside them, until they no longer see gentle people who are no longer gentle writhing in their presumed justice in a building created by those who are not responsible for that same justice but only a story of it, told by a narrator charming, measured, captivating. But never predictable again

in streets like by those closest to very little nothing at all so there can be only you and I traveling down them in the absence of memory, in the absence of any story not belonging to us when we live in the aberrant, self-loathing city which stands furthest away from us, you draw your hands to my chest in the picture of a dance hall refusing its secrets but sharing them all the same when you are released outside, a kiss to build a dream on, a song sings without its might for anyone to hear who remains in its etiquette, polite, unerring, limitable or illuminated, regretting its own circumstances that it reaches you, and it wants to apologize to you, it wants to say that it is sorry for everything you must find before your feet touches the ice because it says your feet will never leave the ice again, not while a narrative remains to keep you there in a building you will never leave while the gentle man who is no longer a gentle man is alive with the memory of a bloody anonymous thumb-print remains in his possession, and not ours

this dream in the night of a name which will not sign itself, the voice which speaks not of you when you and I descend but when a building is entered in the manner of Gary Oldman as Sid Vicious walking through a plate-glass door thinking not of Nancy Spungen but the idea of Nancy Spungen as a client, unworthy of remembrance, unworthy of dreams, and hence the impossibility of the afterlife reunion, of the aborted desires of Nancy Spungen waiting, pacing, but not contemplating on the rooftop of a twelve-story building she has entered with the help of proper etiquette the night sky, the demands of herself to find the ur-friend to release her from the burden of existence boiled down to a series of bloody anonymous thumb-prints people in another building took from her for prostitution or narcotics or forgery or other indiscreet roles frowned upon, not to be claimed by blood but by the limit of the body as it considers its own name and finds it lacking, its faults, imperfections and weaknesses which would remain unclaimed until Gary Oldman knew the vessel of Sid Vicious was all the reclamation humanity needed in a movie to spare the world another bloody anonymous thumb-print outside the Gehry Museum that could be your famous sister's in another story signing in a dream the waiting of unworthy souls you cross paths with while you may wait awhile to stoop down and ask their names and bear witness to how one who suffers, offers.

EXECUTION LETTERS

WHEN I SAY there is always another country far from ours—but not too far, in an anecdotal manner of speaking narrative without actually speaking it—the thought of it brings another day, though not this particular one. Not today, you implore, pushing the letter down in my hands, forgetting you and I already know what it says. These would be the words

where people who were never gentle to begin with who are executed for being anything other than gentle are given no advance notice of the day they are to proceed to the gallows because, say the workers in the building where they reside, they have never deserved anything in advance. Likely never will. Skip the final meal. Last rites waived, padre. Zero-sum gain down the yellow line. Yet the families of these never-gentle people and their next-of-kin and their significant others and every other gentle person in that person who was never gentle to begin with's life receive no advance notice as well. There is only a letter after the fact, or the supposed constructed fact, one that is composed in plain, brusque whiteness, and written by someone working in a building for too long who never knew the person who was never gentle to begin with beyond his or her ill repute. This worked-over working person informs these gentle people waiting elsewhere that the person who was never gentle to begin with had his or her sentence carried out, has been cremated with ashes and other insistent remains scattered at an indeterminate and forever undisclosed location on this particular date and this letter, which is not signed by whomever grants authority, will be only thinnest proof received outside the building of the sentence carried out against mortal body and immutable soul of the deceased the building affixes its imprimatur upon, thinking itself to be the final building because, in many ways, it is, so it has no misgivings of this since everyone has to have a building to call home and people who were never gentle to begin with have been shown they cannot live without a building, even in the afterlife reunion if there is indeed one. It is difficult to be certain of such things here without any anecdotal evidence to assuage you.

Here we are, then—

returning the I say they say,

our condolences again that never are condolences though inquiries of sentimental nature may be directed to this address and phone number during regular weekday business hours unless they are actual inquiries in which case we will not answer since no authority of confirmation exists within this building we choose to work in and sometimes call home sincerely,

yet it is not enough to see it happening in a letter narrated with no foreseeable end. You would rather see him instead since you know you will never see her again. You will only get to keep hearing about her.

Except the another day arrives where you and I and the another day are no longer allowed to enter the building where the gentle man who is no longer a gentle man resides. The people who work at the building no longer require anything of us to allow our entry, other than out of simple etiquette, and upon granting our entry keep us waiting and waiting while you listen to The Sex Pistols for another day on your latest personal technology, and I consider yet again which working person will come out and tell us again what you and I already know.

Another letter that begins arriving for us, already has.

You and I fail to mention to this working person we already know this letter will not be a letter of the classic disposition, regardless of whether it's handwritten or typed, thoughtfully or thoughtlessly composed, being composed in an anti-social language by an admirer who has awaited the moment to arrive and, finding it, this admirer seizes it, taking you by surprise as you rip open each envelope at the top with a pair of heavy fabric scissors, expecting something equally as heavy to fall out, recalling another certain person who was never gentle to begin with's words, Perhaps I will send you something wet. Sorry, old boy, no. It's dry. All so very desertbone dry. Not even a crude salutation but immediately launching into an invective against your famous sister, that she wasn't really as famous as she let on to him, that she wasn't even your sister in the more cruel sense, more and more making vulgar reference to the female anatomy in any number of ways, mostly out of the sort of detachment that comes from writing about things one never knows for certain about or wishes to know— which is the point, of course. Not caring about your famous sister's anatomy. Not caring that the black boy you work with has left the eternal curse from his lips upon the crown of your head. Not caring that it has been three weeks five days since I touched your body on our sofa.

The I knows there will be day when he will be gone, I would tell you here on the sofa.

I know the gentle man who is no longer a gentle man who now knows me—he who knows me better than you—and I will be gone.

Knowing you will know this someday yourself, without me telling you, without the gentle man who is no longer a gentle man, without him reminding you that you had a famous sister once who you knew and was better than me, better for you. You know that without me the gentle man who is no longer a gentle man will be better off for not having any anecdotes told about him, for not knowing what has become of me. Someday I will know this for myself implicitly, intensely, but not personally. You will tell me—if you do not write me—that you and I are better off without each other to remind ourselves of gentle people who are no longer gentle, who would be better off without buildings to make them gentle to the lightest anecdote of their lives to tell for the example of others, the same buildings you and I must leave if we are ever to leave each other for the afterlife reunion.

That is why I tell you about the building the gentle man who is no longer a gentle man must leave only once did once he met your famous sister. And then I will go with him.

*

Lack of reason abounds, they say in one room after the next. There is no reason for you to be in this room. There is no reason for you to be in this building. There is no reason for you to talk to the people working in this building. There is no reason for you to be concerned with the gentle man who is no longer a gentle man in this building. There is no reason for you to be concerned about people who were never gentle in any building. Ripeness is all, all is madness. Go home and try not to gouge your eyeballs out, please. We'll do what we can here, which is what we have been doing up to present, in case you haven't noticed yet.

I have said there is no reason for us to be in the aberrant, self-loathing city as well but to tend to our own work, our hypothetical employment, our exorbitant cohabitation scheme, our questionable livelihood, or, I should say, I tend to your immutable soul often if there is indeed one, thoroughly, discreetly, but not directionally, sending you on menial tasks required of an overworked social worker who must ask about so-and-so non-famous person though no one knows this person anyways, and no one will actually know since the building traffics in no real knowledge but various accountings of lives conspicuously rendered for never-ending perusal in the building and your continued employment. Maybe an occasional anecdote about the black boy can be found. Sometimes I feel at a loss over whether I am actually employed to do anything, much less this. Often I remind myself the gentle man who is no longer a gentle man held far better employment than myself before he met your famous sister. Did that occur to your famous sister, her luck. Was he that shallow to fall in with her, thinking he would have her well-provided for or have himself a gentle woman of some stature at the building he worked at, unlike yourself, unlike yourself with me—an upstate sibling rivalry in the most basic sense, to be sure, but one that precluded an questionable livelihood once *Sid and Nancy* had its way with you and your famous sister and its tragicomical ethos of connubial living measured out as one room-stay intervals in hasty, dirty spoonfuls ringed with little bubbles of heaviest air which whispered Gary Oldman's name when they burst.

There is a different letter for you to write that takes much effort, a development you find strange in this day and age of latest personal technology, that anyone sends any kind of handwritten or typed letter. Yet here they are: formal, informative, but not satisfying. Letters regarding the status of the gentle man who is no longer a gentle man, what the people in the building are doing about him, the procedural etiquette now working its way through the system and how would we continue to receive these updates as they become available, though you and I feel there are no real updates but only the announcement of etiquette unrelated to bloody thumb-prints and the possibility, however remote, of Gary Oldman quitting his employment and entering our exorbitant cohabitation scheme and questionable livelihoods as ur-friend and financial benefactor, to convince the gentle man who is no longer a gentle man to do the right thing and rescind his grasp on Sid Vicious. We can only be who we were meant to play, I imagine Gary Oldman berating him, and Sid Vicious has clearly been beyond your abilities—meager as they are—unlike myself, mate, so why don't you quit the charade [pronounced *sha-rahd* in a deep British inflection his stereotyping has never lost] and let these nice gentle people mourn for that woman whom I met in Los Angeles outside the Gehry Museum and signed her AUTOGRAPHS book despite that she was bleeding head to toe and a loony to boot.

You and I are waiting for this final letter. For the release. Everything leads to the final letter from the last building you and I will ever enter. We know there is someone who will not come out. Everything leads to the end of updates. But the failed etiquette will continue longer than the gentle men and gentle women themselves who insist upon it.

In the in the days delayed leading up to the delayed leading up to the omnipotence of the building no person who was never gentle leaves, you sit and you sit and write a letter to the gentle man who is no longer a gentle man—that is that a letter you a letter you plan to give to the people in the building where is he is so they may give it to him they may give it to him in a friendly reciprocity of etiquette for the letter he gave you concerning the letter he gave you concerning your famous sister which showed he was no longer concerned he was no longer concerned with the days leading up to him entering a building he would he would never leave like Gary Oldman as Sid Vicious walking out of a building for one last for one last slice of pizza before the afterlife reunion with someone whom he thinks is Nancy whom he thinks is Nancy Spungen but will be your famous sister if nothing else can be believed nothing else can be believed about a movie most people consider to be of little cultural import, but it is difficult for the gentle man who is no longer a gentle man to write letters like this in this building he must leave someday because there is no such delay. He hadn't written these kind of letters at his hypothetical employment in the building with the stairwell that lead to the roof of the building where your famous sister waited before meeting your famous sister and watching *Sid and Nancy* over and over, having no audience for himself to narrate to while the people in this building prepare him to leave it forever, that perhaps these are very important words he is about to write for someone's entertainment or edification or both if not his own—no, decidedly not his own, he decides—assuming they make their way to the latest personal technology sponsored by Gary Oldman, leaving him a twinge in his leg, a contraction in his chest, a small smile in the dark he avoids waiting for someone to come along to remind him it's lights out and to tend to cultivating the dream of the bloody thumb-print he will leave on the letter, he will leave, though he knows nothing about what Sid Vicious wrote in letters left in his leather jacket pockets about the world and eternity. Which is unfortunate since it would likely help him articulate his thoughts a little better.

The sequence of dreams, nonsequentially arranged, involves variations upon the letter. During what day was it written, were multiple drafts involved, did your famous sister suggest writing you a letter, and so forth. Your dreaming of the letter has not provided solutions to the thumb-print and the ownership of the blood upon which it sealed the gentle man's signature. The people inside the building are not overly concerned with that since they have evidence and confession, but not a profile of his lack of etiquette. It is a shame they have to kill him, they said observing etiquette, for he has uniqueness and disguises and a self-restraint they have never seen before, not even in their wildest dreams of millions of violent alcoholics with no buildings to call their own, of ten thousand plate-glass doors shattering in unison to the sound of dramatic classical music. Your nonsequential dreams, to be read nonsequentially, do have the value of being entertaining or edifying or both when we are in our place watching the thin televisional voices attempt so poorly to entertain us with their news about the gentle man who is no longer a gentle man delivered with deliberate sequentiality and fear of overt confusion when that sequentiality is forced to be broken down into random unconnected events and violate the etiquette of entertainment. It all must be vaguely familiar, at forced distance. It must be polite, even when the etiquette is crude and vulgar. It would never offend us by telling us we could be entertained in other ways, such as our dreams, which hold no answers to unsolved mysteries of our existence but only pull you and I closer together to another dream being dreamt in another building where one does not walk out of while the dreamer dreams that he is Gary Oldman. Yet the gentle man who is no longer a gentle man knows exactly what you and I (not) speak of, carefully putting down his pen and paper as if they were his wayward grandchildren, and proceeds to tell us about buildings even you and I have never heard of, where people who were never gentle who are in them follow no protocol or etiquette, where even the impulses of an aberrant, self-loathing city are negated and calmed into the unlikeliest of behaviors every gentle man and gentle woman follow. He tells us to be careful of them all, himself included, because these are buildings we cannot avoid entering another day—no more than we can avoid the afterlife reunion—where all transgressions are forgiven, where all the people who were never gentle suddenly become gentle as though they were replaced with other gentle people who can no longer recognize what is gentle anymore.

Waiting for the day to arrive he will never know, the gentle man who is no longer a gentle man, in the final building he will never leave, paces in the room he will never leave until the day arrives when someone knocks on his door, telling him he must leave. He never receives visitors. He never writes anything. He never talks until the people in the building instruct him to talk, and even then there is little for him to say, yet, he thinks, he would better off not saying that little thing there is to say.

In this room he inhabits I grant him the boon of introspection. Out of deference to your famous sister, I make sure that introspection is only connected to his sense of Gary Oldman as Sid Vicious while he mulls over his own form of withdrawal, the shakes which come from needing an extra blanket at night and from any other need connected to a certain algebra he has never known for himself in his former gentleness.

You and you all may wonder if it occurs to him that he is in this predicament because of a movie he had watched over and over and over with your famous sister, and that an interruption provided by my possible knocking on a door in the building he lived in with your famous sister may have provided the opportunity he needed to, like, you know, snap out of it, and realize everything he needed to know about your famous sister and the potential tragicomic ethos of connubial living watching *Sid and Nancy* repeatedly, frequently, but not passively would engender but never provided for him in every sense of the word. It does. I also grant him a certain measure of repetition and reiteration and revision to consider how the interruption, all interruptions, may save him from the day he will never know, if not me, specifically, of course, since he can never know or be aware of me in any capacity, not even as the lowly narrator of his annotated story which knows only one life while he remains in this building,

the problem being he believes he had something of a life, if you will, with your famous sister, a life that commenced with the opening scene of *Sid and Nancy* with Sid sitting in the building and never ended with the afterlife reunion commenced in the taxi cab as it sped away while being serenaded by black boys, and that the serenade stops becoming facetious as soon as Gary Oldman as Sid Vicious enters the driverless taxi cab made him believe he was living this life with your famous sister, but only when rewinding the videotape and playing *Sid and Nancy* again and playing *Sid and Nancy* again and playing *Sid and Nancy* again and never knowing the end, he realizes, because Alex Cox had created a movie that would never end in 1986 contingent upon no one knocking on the door outside which would interrupt the tragicomic ethos forever of Gary Oldman as Sid Vicious sitting on the mattress with knife in hand and your famous sister as Nancy on the bathroom floor and him wondering what the bloody hell happened

and the more the gentle man who is no longer a gentle man paces in his room, the more certain he grows of this.

He fails to explain this growing certainty to the people in the building. He knows this much, at least, that they would never believe him about anything—much like how you will never really believe me about anything—never see his mouth moving while he and they wait for the another day they will never know to arrive

*

when it arrives may have a sound a sound which interrupts him from the
nothing he is doing, waiting for the nothing outside his door to interrupt him,
to call him out from the auspices of your famous sister, knowing only there
is a door to be knocked upon, calling him back out into the hallway where
anecdotal experience is born, a call unto perpetuity thinking he would care to
rejoin the world of gentle people and partake of their etiquette, perhaps even
knock on doors himself to call these other people out and say to them, Hello,
you've never met me but I'm as gentle as you are, so let's go make anecdotes
together before the afterlife reunion—only, he can see, the confusion on their
faces since they have never seen *Sid and Nancy* nor are aware of its cultural
significance, even when put into context of Gary Oldman's long, successful
acting career, nor likely have been violent alcoholics themselves or come from
violent alcoholic families or have had a sibling try to drown them in a bathtub
of scalding water

at that slinking away from them,

escape always looks easy, it may occur to him, when the other person
knows there is no one else to return to, which he does not

standing in his room heading to the door the only door available to him
the only door he could possibly walk through but won't, not until the day he
doesn't know arrives, calling him by a name he has long forgotten by now
because your famous sister never had occasion to actually ask him about it,
but he will tell the people in this building his name now, at night, drawing his
hand up to gently rap, knocking his

knocking on the other side of a door, the inside knocking which knocks a
door of the door upon the inside knock, another door where there is no knocking
either inside or outside, a door's knock coming from inside a knocker where no
door is in front but a knocking instead outside on a door in another building
where, inside, knocking doors cause the door itself to appear for not only the
knocker knocking but the building itself, the inside itself created from the
knocking which all knockers need to enter (or ask to enter—which is all they
can ever really do), regardless of whether they stand inside or outside doors of
their choosing, thinking themselves inside when they hear the knock so there is
no outside but the inside coming from their knock being created upon the door,
pointing themselves to an inside where there are no doors finally because there
are no buildings finally but only the absence of knocking for a door coming
inside, a knock on the knocking, a knock inside the knocking which creates

a door for another to knock upon so that the inside knocking can be another building outside where there are no doors to knock upon.

The day can only come as it does when the gentle man who is no longer a gentle man is gone. They say. You and I are the only ones who are notified of this. There are no friends. No family. No subscription plan will ever be satisfied. You will never be satisfied for having not seen him before.

The letter says, in its own furthermore which you ignore along with myself, he has stayed in the building, any building, long enough for anyone's satisfaction of the duration and duress of the stay, but now no longer welcome to stay another day, having no more information to purse and peruse, having no more etiquette they themselves can impart, having all questions answered except those regarding the whereabouts and the intrinsic nature of your famous sister, the latter of which cannot be answered by *Sid and Nancy* since Gary Oldman is unavailable for comment and is currently en-route to shooting a commercial for the latest personal technology and won't be making statements anytime soon, especially because the people in the building have no need to talk to him or anyone connected to *Sid and Nancy*, such as the gentle man who is no longer a gentle man. Who is no longer here.

Until the day comes that the words of the gentle man who is no longer a gentle man have a growing interest in the public-at-large, many of them lonely from the absence of ur-friends in their life, and they ask, Where are these words of the gentle man who is no longer a gentle man, why have we not seen them, we have good money to spend on these words, money we have earned through countless hours of subjecting ourselves to etiquette in a building— sometimes many buildings—and we want to know we want to know we want to knowewantoknowewant whatever it is was the gentle man who is no longer a gentle man wanted in his life. Since it was not your famous sister, which, I may say, he had all the same. It is more likely she kept him and prodded him and rolled herself into a tight ball on his lap as the video repeated and the drinks were poured and she told him during the bore-reen interludes of the movie about what she hoped for herself upstate which, she confessed, was not a gentle man but a long series of signatures as a possible video installation project to ultimately sell to the Gehry Museum in Los Angeles if it existed so that the building would finally exist and that she could walk through the doors like Gary Oldman as Sid Vicious, videotaped (but not recorded) by someone she had not decided on yet—maybe him, he has steady hands—and then add a supplemental making-of video to enhance the experience of endless names, all of them famous and would-be famous, all of them from her AUTOGRAPHS book that you refuse to burn.

Except for a signature. The one. The name you know. The name she would keep for herself. Even keep from him next to her who I picture nodding off just as the bobbies assail the party boat on the Thames for the ten-thousandth raid and two people who are never gentle and never will be stroll away unscathed from rioting on the dock, shoulder to shoulder, oblivious to it all and breathing it in yet again.

THE ASSASSIN'S
COFFEE BREAK

THIS DAY OF ALL DAYS when I presumed getting a cup of my
favorite coffee from one of my favorite chain coffee shops, an act alone which
compels self-loathing for many anecdotal decisions made on my part for your
entertainment or edification or both, I saw a sign inside the shop advertising
one of the favorite chain's new blends carefully created in tandem with the
rapidly changing weather patterns in A Celebration of the Passage of Time.

Since Time does whatever it wants to and most people never grow happy
with it when it does, I couldn't resist asking my favorite anecdotal barista
from Louisiana, who resembles in a distant way Gary Oldman as Lee Harvey
Oswald from Oliver Stone's *JFK*, for a celebratory cuppa. Once, maybe just
once, I could feel the famous assassin's full joy of having Time with me, on
my side, my very best ur-friend who I have unfortunately neglected up until
now because of this matter of your famous sister, despite that you yourself
always serve as a sufficient distraction from the vicissitudes of ever-encroaching
Time which the acting career of Gary Oldman reminds me of more these
days, he who moves further away from the blissless, redundant nihilism of
Lee Harvey Oswald and into more colorless roles requiring starched shirts
and Windsor knot ties and CGI and product placement for the latest personal
technology. With Time on my side, then, I will forgive Time for doing that
to him. Since I could never be Gary Oldman as Lee Harvey Oswald while

drinking coffee, Gary Oldman could never be me if I were ever to become a famous enough assassin to deserve a product placement for a past, uncredited role, a role showing how I watched a second-hand VHS copy of *JFK* with your famous sister at your civil servant parents' house upstate over and over as she kept pausing the tape frame by frame to stare at his arms in those Southern short-sleeves. Time, like her fetishizing Zapruderism, like an erotic celluloid Oswald, is working both for and against me with each sip of coffee I now take, its Guatemalan floral tones evoking a calm summer breeze in my increasingly narratological nose I press against the window for our upstairs neighbor passing by on the sidewalk to notice, my motioning to have her join me inside with that perpetual sad smile she always wears in the basement laundry room.

Upon this sacrificial and semi-allegorical non-gesture of mine, I am reminded not of Maurice Blanchot but of Thomas Merton instead, another upstate refugee she has told me about, whose body was buried uncovered in coarse linen soaked with the usual blood and urine and other fluids when he was done with it, as was the custom where he lived. Before Time had its way with him, he sat writing somewhere in that upstate monastery, making money for those brothers who wanted money as they slapped and kicked each other while he watched and took note. This was perhaps in the same grudging way your famous sister and I watched *JFK* repeatedly but without the faith in Jesus that Merton or even Kennedy likely applied in saintly resolve—the same resolve needed to drink this coffee with our upstairs neighbor approaching— against Time and all its lonely perverts casting lonely eyes, subservient, as she and I were, to the muted violent impulses of Gary Oldman as Lee Harvey Oswald which knew no hand but only guided by influence. Resolving to never resolve is still a resolution, Time responds, even if Merton will never be canonized, even if your famous sister and I never reach the true end of *JFK*, even if the lonely perverts never shed a single tear for suffering torment. This torment of writing Merton knew himself all too well thanks to Time and influence and coffee, commingled in unequal and inexact amounts thanks to the good brothers, claims our upstairs neighbor while seated next to me with a manuscript she has wanted to show me spilling out from her satchel on the oversmall pseudo-table.

Merton had something like Time on his side if not his writing, she continues explaining to me while enjoying her own celebratory coffee, dying as young as he had. Dying to be left uncovered. His body releasing its foul liquids, absorbed by the coarse cloth which the order required, all with the implication of isolating violence it carried for Merton by association if not sheer influence, tactile or otherwise. She believes he understood this cloth would not cover him in actual death but only the living death, the solemn price paid for eventual veneration if not benediction. So he had heard all these stories before. Wrote a few of them down. Then went to sleep dreaming of the death of gentle men as the order also required because of Time. But it was better to write, no matter how much it made one into a lonely pervert rebuffing the overtures of Jesus, lain heavily against the inopportune arrhythmia once called a *heart* by better poets than he in their violence unfulfilled.

How terrible to work out all specifics of a body, neglecting what it comes down to: either someone dies gently, or someone dies violently. The manner of death by Time, its own violence without pausing so much as once, recorded in *JFK*, and the coarse linen of Oliver Stone then absorbs the foul liquids, offensive as they are, bristling against our gentle sensibilities as Gary Oldman's on-screen psychopathy does. Writers are always smelling each other if not themselves. Which, I suppose, is why our upstairs neighbor prefers sidling up to me instead of you. Writers are always allowing themselves to be smelled,

her voice next to me interrupts my thought of your famous sister and commingles her with Merton, the most unfortunate pairing I could think of beyond Sid Vicious and Nancy Spungen, Oswald and Kennedy, Dracula and Mina, Stansfield and Matilda, Rosencrantz and Guildenstern, or yourself and the black boy,

if they don't smell what they want to, she goes on while further recalling from her notable literary education a certain modern Japanese protagonist's fascination with a Russian woman he dances with, later obsessing over the lingering smell of her sweat on his hands as exotica. But, she adds, the smell he takes is only solitary, and private, and away from the supposed conversant. I put down my coffee and welcome the silence of the patrons around us watching. This indirect apology from her for not making the necessary etiquette of eye contact with me only satisfies me up to a point (much like watching *JFK*) before she puts down her coffee as well, drawing her nose close to my left temple, and starts sniffing.

THE SADNESS OF THE GENTLE WOMAN WITH THIRTEEN UNPUBLISHED NOVELS

IN A SINGLE, SOLITARY room on the floor above us in the building where you and I live resides the sadness of the gentle woman who has written twelve novels and a thirteenth that may or may not belong to Maurice Blanchot, but never had any of them published.

There are always many reasons for a writer of novels to remain unpublished, but our upstairs neighbor's reasons remain atypical as I attempt to understand them in my narrative interference of overt sympathy and bathos—another failed etiquette, as it were. Because no one has ever helped alleviate her sadness, not a single gentle person in a favorite chain coffee shop. Not even herself. Not even while possibly ghost writing for Maurice Blanchot who she claims to have met, and known. Like, that known, you say. Another case study in overcompensating chronic despondency for the office, I interject as you grab the laundry basket and leave to make your customary descent into the basement where you know you do not want to run into her, but there is always so much laundry to be done as I wait to hear from Los Angeles about the I. I say to you ignoring me and halfway out the door, then, it can't be helped, like most helpless narrators in their ineffectual way while Gary Oldman makes up his mind about me.

Among the many reasons why I don't write novels.

*

The sadness of this gentle woman upstairs should commence, much like other gentle women, with a more private stock than your famous sister's, where my hand on her door at night cannot penetrate through and render her thin voices as either televisional or radiological since she forsakes all forms of technology earliest and latest. Thus her voices fall downstairs to the basement of my mind where all the lonely perverts lying on the ground gather to complain of the gentle people whom they cannot hear and imagine for themselves as you and I, I imagine, look and tsk-tsk them, nudging an impolite, jabbering head aside with our feet while we continue, aware of neither ascent nor descent but remaining all the same with those who are lost, wondering what exactly are they doing with themselves here when we don't notice them.

To remain in a room forever is to be both lost and not-lost, our upstairs neighbor will tell us gently when you and I happen to find her doing laundry in the basement. This is the room where all the great writers of the last century must and have indeed written in, such as Maurice Blanchot, she says with a discernible sigh, after he attempted one last manuscript under the conditioning of a failed American etiquette for once in his life, the novel that she claims to have written over and over and finish until a hairless agent would accept it but never did. You and I know better than to ask her to see this thirteenth novel because that is what all writers secretly desire when in public: springing the trap of sharing. But you and I, attuned to this unrequited sadness of hers, do not feel the desire to encourage this behavior after the example of the gentle man who is no longer a gentle man, whose shared letter announcing what had happened to your famous sister is the ice our feet still tread upon as our upstairs neighbor's words soothe and honey our ears over while her delicates spin and turn in a deliberate, gentle heat until they find their appropriate level of dryness.

Often an appropriate level of dryness can be found in a hypothetical unpublished translated novel by Maurice Blanchot that the gentle woman does not publish for the thirteenth Time in her life. You have wondered if Gary Oldman, having to write his signature over and over again in an AUTOGRAPHS book for anyone who attempts to walk through plate-glass doors, felt this dryness in his mouth while waiting for your famous sister at the Gehry Museum to find a pen in her purse with her unharmed hand, felt the sadness of himself as another Gary Oldman forced by etiquette to write his signature over and over again, much to the disproval of a hairless agent hovering nearby. And when handing back both the pen and the

AUTOGRAPHS book to your famous sister, did he feel the stickiness of her blood as it moved her fingers, the soothing, honeyed words of her admiration and disbelief of finding him in front of the Gehry Museum which exists only in his mind when he walks into the basement of his home to do his laundry, which may or may not include delicates. If the delicates of Gary Oldman are stained, however—such as, for instance, by the blood of your famous sister— does he walk out of that basement the same Gary Oldman who signed his own name, or a different Gary Oldman, one who returns to his room, alone, to consider the sign of your famous sister which compels him to write a novel or varying lengths and styles so that the stain may be lifted from his delicates, or transferred, that is, to another delicate which may never please him or his hairless agent or anyone else but that he stores away in his desk nonetheless so he may later partake in the sadness of a room he knows he will never leave.

The sadness of our upstairs neighbor who says she has written twelve unpublished novels prevents her from knowing for certain what to do with this thirteenth manuscript of an appropriate dryness, she had told me, but that she is considering giving it to an old man with yellowish white hair at my favorite chain coffee shop because he looks like a heavily aged Gary Oldman and because he understands a thing or two about Maurice Blanchot, I am told, though not necessarily much about waiting and the eternal. In fact, she says, he claims his life has never been touched by violence in any way shape or form or even the formlessness of reading and hearing about violence, which makes me wonder if this old man is indeed the product of an aberrant, self-loathing city, like your black boy at the social building and his eternal curse. Her wanting to give him a bloody anonymous thumb-print on a porcelain shard she does not possess could be construed as the most violent thing which has ever happened to him while living here. Soon she feels appropriately, instinctively, but not kindly that I would be better off in possession of the thirteenth manuscript rather than an old man with yellowish hair who looks like a heavily aged Gary Oldman if only because, unlike yourself, I believe her about Maurice Blanchot even if no one else will. I believe an unpublished manuscript could be the product of Maurice Blanchot even if he never actually wrote it. I believe a bloody anonymous thumb-print at the end of a letter cannot forever remain anonymous while you and I search for the closest thing to Jesus in our perverted lives.

Yet I also note the sadness of the old woman living above us who has written twelve novels but never published any of them leaves her strangely unfamiliar with the tragedy of Sid Vicious eating pizza alone in the afterlife. She will protest about not liking pizza to begin with. That's no reason for a person who loves pizza to be denied company in the afterlife, I make her recognize, even if his famous name alone suggests he is not at all a gentle man. A writer like herself has only ever kept the company of gentle men, and many of those would forswear pizza if it meant keeping her company indefinitely, a gentle woman of much taste and intelligence. Maurice Blanchot had never eaten so much as a single hot slice during his stay in New York, so she found it was easy for him to give up pizza when they were together working on translating his final manuscript. Which is better than working alone. Which is better than eating alone. Which is better than spending forever in the afterlife alone. Which is better than being Sid Vicious, I suppose.

Is it better than being Gary Oldman being Sid Vicious. I am not entirely sure. Since she likely knows very little about the work of Gary Oldman given her deficiency in Sid Vicious lore, I have difficulty broaching this subject with her. Apropos of *Sid and Nancy*, I do ask if she thinks if there is an afterlife reunion in store between her and Maurice Blanchot, acknowledging, too, that Blanchot probably did not believe in an afterlife, and if he was there, he was likely being held against his will in a building all-too accustomed to writers such as himself. She is aware of this and smiles at me first, condescendingly, patronizingly, but not amusingly. She thinks I have besmirched her beautiful Maurice with my blatant fact-killing, not so much for seeing through her professional, eroticized relationship with Blanchot and finding those secret desires which make all the sense in the world to seasoned narrators such as myself, yet confuse the reticence to speak about it with a possible resentment for exposing something which does not need to be exposed.

This reticence which I let manifest for her in different forms in our building has its usefulness, but only when laundry is involved, only when the etiquette of laundry in a semi-public laundry room anticipates the sort of anecdotal behavior which Maurice Blanchot would have never cared for. He himself would be the kind of gentle man to care for a sad, old woman who, no longer feeling compelled to work on a fourteenth unpublished novel, spends most of her Time doing laundry in the basement, dividing it into lights and darks compulsively, obsessively, but not endlessly. So much laundry to be done for a solitary old woman who does nothing but remain sad upstairs. She has Maurice Blanchot to thanks for this, she believes. Having read something by him that was not exactly a novel in the conventional or contrived sense while in graduate school for some meandering professor she cannot remember now out of etiquette's sake, our upstairs neighbor feels Blanchot was the best influence her own writing encountered in the utter whiteness of having to write out page after page with the earliest personal technology (forever eschewing the latest personal technology, including gentle Italian typewriters) which her meandering professor's behest stays, her fountain pen drawing still to his having her wrist complete a line incomplete, as she meant it, meant for Maurice Blanchot, that is, she thought then, the first Time she had done so. She certainly couldn't tell him or him or anyone else or everyone else, not while her meandering professor watched every page passing under his glance, looking for a him, not finding it amongst this one, he saw, and deciding all the same. She knew well enough. Nothing well enough comes from such advance. Everything under her was to be his, and she was never allowed to believe any of it. All right, then. Easier not to believe. She whom I speak of when you and I do not see her, when guided down the hallway of myriad voices behind doors, is left to wonder about her fellow graduates forever writing novels under professors unseen, a promise to handle the whiteness, to take care of it, she thinks Maurice Blanchot would say could she imagine what his voice sounds like. Except she can't. Not anymore. Not even while reading his writing in the original French, as though putting her hand to a door and hearing the thin reverberations of a building unaccustomed to the sounds it makes, whether in form of televisional or radiological voices, violent alcoholic protests, gentle promises made under guise of not being gentle, thinking, How could such a building stand with such people in it who refuse hearing these things. She eventually understood that they do hear but only if the building itself disappears in the same manner of a gentle person who is no longer gentle. She saw the meandering professor thusly, taking care not to mention these voices to him, this Maurice Blanchot who stood between him and her. A building was always around her where someone else who was everyone else could hear everything that a gentle person didn't want to hear, and more. It was then she began to feel sorry for Maurice Blanchot. He would have to hear all of this in the hallway, the meandering professor, her, the voices of a failed etiquette raining upon his head while he tried to write without a single story to fragment in the design of incompleteness in deliberation, and all the writing to be done in a building, all the whiteness succumbing to overcome but does not, all and all and all. There was no escape. Only the building. Only the diversions it represented and divided and kept tucked away from public view—or so it thought—much like the motion of her hand at work too late for the meandering professor's liking, until, that is, he left her apartment the following morning, out the front door with a whistle. She never heard this whistle, and yet. She likened its being there to what Maurice Blanchot's voice would sound like if, for instance, he lived just down the hallway from her and, at night, her wandering to his door to discover what happens when he writes under the guise of a gentle man who has always been gentle, never concerned about his whiteness slipping out of his room unbeknownst to him with a sense of its own sadness for its association with a Maurice Blanchot who could stand an ur-friend in his life. Perhaps two, even. That's a lot to ask for, she realized, finding her lights and darks thoroughly intertwined and co-mingled, which, to be sure, the meandering professor remains somewhat responsible for to this day. Such is the reason laundry rooms are good places to whistle in, especially when no gentle people are around separating their lights and darks. Once you had caught her downstairs, you confessed, whistling a tune that vaguely resembled Anarchy in the U.K. in spite of its low pitch and slower, more somber delivery, surprising both her and you as you glided into the room (some thoughtful, gentle person had jammed the wooden triangle into the doorframe in a rare observance of etiquette) to find a gentle old woman mournfully conveying a Sex Pistols tune over a heap of battered, rumpled clothing that seemed as ancient as ten thousand photo albums with no photos in them, her tune drawing to a complete stand-still while you stood waiting for her to clear the only table in the room so you could place your basket on it. I'm almost finished, dear, she told you instead, though you could plainly see she was nowhere near finished. Just some gentle thing to say to someone much younger, less gentle. A deferred bitchiness, you thought. Then you noticed it was dark there in the basement, the light only coming in from barred windows high and close to the ceiling, with evening soon approaching and this woman in no particular hurry. The etiquette of interruption, however, prevented you from withdrawing back upstairs to me and explaining all this. Patience. Waiting. The course of action through inaction. Laundry would never get done otherwise. Yet as you stood with a full basket while she delineated your presence through the act of sorting, you wondered if she really ever wanted her laundry done, sensing its importance was only secondary to having you wait and understand why she was whistling in the dark something she should not be whistling given her apparent gentleness with age and lack of publishing success. Conversation was out of the question. Maurice Blanchot would have never approved: merely an exchange of trite anecdotes, mostly about your famous sister, which she has already heard or read about in the earliest personal technology's late metro edition. The deliberate act of a gentle man who is no longer a gentle man won't make her go any faster. She had learned that. It frightened her in a way, having to watch the meandering professor read every single page of her first complete manuscript in his office while she sat facing away from the window, not knowing how slowly the day was passing until a kind of darkness suggested itself upon his crenellated scowl and her finding that she had disappeared altogether from her waiting and re-emerged into a small tune in her head that spontaneously, impulsively, but not respectfully she started whistling in front of him, no more than halfway through her work, finally drawing his eyes up off it to meet hers, and knowing his attention was truly hers let the whistled song grow louder for his recognition of its origin, the circumstances of its composition, the untold influences which reigned over its creation, and the mouth which wielded all of these, fleshy, unbecoming, oh so gentle. Am I bothering you, dear, she finally asked, you propping up your full basket on sore hip, I must've forgotten where I am. A sentiment you concurred with before finding the switch and flooding the basement with florescent light upon the sharp jab of your elbow. Her hands darted away. I should really put these in now, she said, and, while grabbing the lights pile first with both arms to direct it towards an empty machine, she politely asked about you and whether you are a writer though you said no, but told her instead that I was, in a way, no, not really, you supposed, as she then put the darks pile in the same machine as the lights, dispensed detergent, fished for some quarters in her pocket, and sent the entire load to spin and churn itself wet which you watched with a seething intensity for all your waiting to see these lights and darks mixed again until the two piles lose their shape, their limit in this machine, in this basement, in the mind of our upstairs neighbor prone to whistling to herself in the dark while no one reads any of her twelve unpublished novels.

In that case, she told you in a wisp, in a warning, too—I'll have to show you two this thirteenth manuscript I helped an ur-friend with, as she took her empty basket and cleared out, leaving the only table to you alone, including a catchy dirge in your head to fend off.

AT THE HOTEL CHELSEA,
YOUR DREAMS ARE ONLY A BODY BAG

WHILE I HAVE HIM writing at the Hotel Chelsea what would be his only unpublished novel, Maurice Blanchot obsesses over an anonymous bloody thumb-print. A thumb-print he finds on the white ceramic coffee cup he drinks from in the lobby during the morning of the commotion. The coffee cup which will sit in his room, unwashed, unwashable. Almost famous.

The obsession I allow him flies in the face of classic etiquette of hospitality. His initial inclination towards this gross violation of it—which is also the first violation of any kind visited upon him in New York—is to return the coffee, even upbraid the front desk in vigorous Parisian fashion, the only fashion he knows. He does neither. He keeps sipping the coffee carefully (still very hot from an unseen carafe which perhaps doesn't exist) so he can continue mulling over the enigma of the thumb-print, whose blood comprised it, and why he has accepted its totality for reasons other than *memento mori* by bringing it back to his room and leaving it on his desk for the duration of his stay.

Cheapness alluring, he thinks. Earliest souvenir.

Maurice Blanchot, author of *Death Sentence* and *Thomas the Obscure*, forced into being a gentle man who may no longer be a gentle man. By a coffee cup. A potential crime scene trinket. This will bother him later as he walks back up three flights of stairs to his room.

This bothers you and you all at present.

A hotel, any hotel, every hotel may be a place where gentle men and gentle women who no longer wish to be gentle reside in a false perpetuity orchestrated by a failed American etiquette itself. The Hotel Chelsea is not that kind of a hotel. It is not any kind of a hotel, as our upstairs neighbor keeps insisting to us.

Unwashed, unwashable. Almost famous.

You do not want to believe this gross violation of etiquette.

Of course you complain the picture I commence developing is doomed to incompleteness without your famous sister's input, who claimed to us once that she had stayed there with someone almost famous, maybe a writer, which was a distinct possibility knowing her. You, on the other hand, never claimed to have stayed there, other than what you experienced as a teenager repeatedly watching *Sid and Nancy* with her. You also have never seen Blanchot's face, relying on descriptions provided by the sighing, aborted desires of our upstairs neighbor in the laundry room and my blatant fact-killing thus far. And the face always construes a powerful device for you, more so than the violent alcoholic acting style of Gary Oldman. More so than a coffee cup with an anonymous bloody thumb-print on it. More so than an idea of the famous Hotel Chelsea I could convey in ten thousand unpublished novels. More so than desire mixed with falsehood from never being there.

But that is how, at least, I may help you recover from the eternal loss of your famous sister: no guest can be satiated at the Hotel Chelsea with a lingering, unconscious desire to write one's self into place for as long as etiquette reigns where none exists, not as long as the aberrant, self-loathing city multiplies itself building by building, fills itself more and more with gentle men who wish they could be the same young man in a black leather jacket whom Blanchot watches being led out in handcuffs through the lobby before the body of a young woman in a thick, black plastic bag is wheeled away on a stretcher, an attending detective leaving a white ceramic coffee cup at the front desk as he exits with the victim.

An hour later, Blanchot will be sipping with care the coffee of dubious actuality he had asked for so that his lips avoid touching the thumb-print.

*

For alleviating your discomfort with anecdotes and the eternal, I may also suggest a very late call made to his room prior to the commotion.

The call is from an initially polite young gentle man who claims to be employed at the hotel without providing a name or even mentioning the front desk—a scenario you are familiar with from your famous sister's many attempts at recreating the Hotel Chelsea experience while you and her lived upstate with your civil servant parents. Blanchot, however, doesn't recognize the set-up, nor the British voice as belonging to anyone downstairs. He eventually understands, as this gentle man who was never a gentle man prattles on about a mistake made with his reservation, that a swindle is being attempted. This amuses Blanchot despite the hour because the person is doing it all wrong. He asks the caller whether he has considered the fundamental inequality of this conversation as it pertains to hospitality etiquette of identifying one's self, of situation, of station and its reciprocity. You do not know my name but know where I am, Blanchot points out in inflected English, which is more than I know about you. The caller admits, in all fairness, this had not occurred to him. He manages to slip in a tersely worded sentiment regarding Blanchot's mental capacity and make vulgar reference to a particularity of the female anatomy before hanging up.

Muttering under his breath why, at this hour, he decides to banter with a half-witted scam artist only looking to chisel ten, maybe twenty American dollars at most from this susceptible guest, a charitable Blanchot begins consulting his own guilt. Then a change of heart when the gentle man who was never a gentle man calls him back, refers to him as Frenchy, and proceeds *non sequitur* into a violent alcoholic diatribe against his lover present in the room, whom Blanchot can hear whining and moaning in the background, drunk if not worse. A tussle ensues for the receiver, supposedly. Dial tone sounds again.

Blanchot decides the fun is over.

The phone jack pulls out with rotted ease from the wall before he drifts off into a dream about a phone jack.

The idea of Blanchot's traveling, leaving France for awhile, takes me a few days of narrating to have it materialize in your thoughts for any number of reasons both you and I are aware of, not the least of these being a general trepidation of a failed American etiquette and becoming a tourist of it. When these two possibilities coalesce, you recoil from me on our sofa in as much pain as the wounding prospect allows, so much so that I almost have him cancel his plane ticket and reservation at the Chelsea, set up for him by a philosopher friend who had stayed there long-term and returned home with much acclaim after his book about the cultural history of Western abnegation was published. Not that the Blanchot you and I know seeks the limelight of cultural import. On the contrary, he may think the Chelsea an opportune way to increase his isolation further, which his work commends him for, in secret, once drinks are poured, once the lights are down, once you and I rest our heads on the ample manuscript given to us by our upstairs neighbor, the pages ready to reward the author if he can find the right vessel for all that is interminable about his life. Or, that is, the sense of his life.

The reasons you and I have for not wanting to visit the Hotel Chelsea are different than Maurice Blanchot's, assuming we believe our upstairs neighbor who knows you and me better than Blanchot, despite a lost weekend spent with Blanchot in Niagara Falls, despite the particulars of her professional relationship with Blanchot, despite that you and I have been told she has twelve unpublished manuscripts and a thirteenth being what he supposedly tried writing at the Hotel Chelsea, despite everything you and I do not know about Maurice Blanchot. Her own particular brand of fact-killing does not involve searching hallways as I am accustomed to in my explorations but is a systematic progression of incremental disclosures only in the laundry room of our building, the number and provided detail determined by the clothes she folds in our presence. You speculate she deliberately employs fabric softener sheets to prompt her memory, a device not unlike Marcel Proust's madeline but closer instead to Jean Genet's inhaling the flatulence embedded in his prison blanket, the more pleasant harshness of the chemical compositions released into the air after the dryer rings its finish-bell. Pouring onto her lap the steaming, vaporous linens of lavender or lilacs, April and May, she will indulge before us her reminiscing, oh, oh, upon Maurice Blanchot's body *après-douche*, especially with that fine Parisian soap he always lathered in, brushing aside her fountainous yellowish white hair at every opportunity.

My narrative, as you and you all know well by now, can only luxuriate in the scent that itself gives off. Blanchot hardly makes one out for himself at the Hotel Chelsea, and he prefers not to take stock of the lobby in this regard, especially as the police roll the body bag away to the people in another building who handle matters like those involving your famous sister. You and I are often aware that most polite hotels smell like our upstairs neighbor's fabric softener, lavender or lilacs, April and May, and then, upon stepping into a room, any room, every room, this scent will fade into some mysterious recess. All Maurice Blanchot can be left with is neutral air, skirted with the unfamiliar scents of its former inhabitants he detects with slight disapproval as various body odors dissipate upon the arrival of a new guest.

The sheer ineptitude of his decision makes Blanchot very glad to be here.

He opens his balcony window. He unpacks and sets up his manual typewriter on the desk, waits for the first admirer to knock on his door and recognize the scent of a Maurice Blanchot fresh out of a Hotel Chelsea shower. Resting on the bed while doing so draws his thoughts into delicate, light sketches of an anonymous Futurist painting of the Brooklyn Bridge he had appreciated in the lobby while checking in, the image slowly decomposing in his evaluations, his room included.

The next hypothetical manuscript does not need the streets of New York. There is no inspiration there, he soon determines, no dialogue pregnant with possibilities, no inspirational characters who ask for characterizing, no anecdote that needs immediate sharing, especially his own. There are only gentle men who may no longer be gentle men, like himself, and gentle women who do not hold open doors for him. He considers whether he has made a terrible mistake. He welcomes the mistake which he has no control over. The only way to live in an aberrant, self-loathing city is to be antagonized by it continuously, frequently, but not endlessly. The terminus of hatred and self-loathing is the unexpected revelation, the empty epiphany which constitutes recognition of the disaster to befall everyone, such as a young woman wheeled out in a body bag. Arriving at this very sane conclusion, he starts feeling better in a Maurice Blanchot kind of way. There is surely a hidden avenue, he thinks. Perhaps he is even involved to some degree with what has happened as he reflects upon the particulars of his phone conversation with the violent alcoholic young man, the annoying voice of the young woman.

The next manuscript needs the rooms of the Hotel Chelsea.

Most of all, our upstairs neighbor adds while folding her suitpants, he remembers that moment his fondness for stories of buildings where nothing appears to happen.

Architecture of every kind sends him around the hotel during the afternoons, counting the number of stairs between the twelve floors, discovering which rooms are the most asked for. His morning typewriting and lobby newspaper reading habits are given a rest as he finds opportunities to commiserate with the almost famous guests, to ask them about the habits of the young couple which caused the recent commotion, and thus confirm the elevated position of this building he harbors great suspicions about. The guests often deflect his inquiries with sidelong glances at the bohemian paintings in the lobby. They are fucking tired of talking about those two cheap assholes, he senses with his imperfect grasp of English in the local *patois*. They would rather view the works of a defied conversational etiquette, by far a more interesting prospect than discussing a broken young man in a black leather jacket whose ten thousand stories now circulating the twelve floors of this hotel and their intellectual circles about his condition in another building wander into the oft-repeated and seldom reliable. Same old fucking shit, they decry, and resign themselves to wait for the inevitable if not justice, which is what you and you all ever really deserve. Blanchot is uncertain if this young couple deserves the inevitable, which is still something like justice. No one really deserves that, if anything. No one can ever punish themselves when the forces beyond their control refuse punishment.

An anonymous bloody thumb-print is a terrible way to be acquainted with a hotel.

A basement room at an alluringly cheap hotel not believing itself to be alluringly cheap where a gentle man who was never a gentle man lives with a gentle woman who was never a gentle woman.

The typing continues for three straight days. No guests enter his room, no one is offered a drink or a few moments of philosophical respite from the world of lobby newspapers—no one, nothing but a manuscript.

He thinks it is inevitable that he won't be leaving for awhile.

Pages start accumulating on the desk, next to the shabby vintage lamp which barely works unless he jiggles the switch repeatedly, next to his watch, his best fountain pen.

An unwashed, unwashable coffee cup sends him ahead the room.

Maurice Blanchot dreams of dead bodies in his room very carefully because this is the room of Maurice Blanchot I am talking about.

He thinks he can hear breathing in (this) dream, slow, insistent, not his own.

There is no dreaming in the way gentle men and gentle women, like you and me, who have never stayed at the Hotel Chelsea dream of dead bodies as horrible and insistent, as though they are friends who left us long ago and now return to provide comfort of the eternal. In the dreams of Maurice Blanchot is an ur-friend for commiseration, and, as such, he dreams of it as the excrescence from his current writing, signed with the seal of an anonymous bloody thumb-print, ten thousand eyebrows raising themselves over the specter of someone he has never known or seen or spoken to up until now, as he places his hand carefully on the thick black plastic, feeling its unforgiving grasp upon the body inside, and the coldest zipper grumbling in its sleep.

Yet the top flap of the body bag is not rising and falling as one would expect a body's lungs to expand and contract in the irrationality of dreams. To help confirm this, he places one hand on the top flap—not to unzip the zipper and look, of course, which would be a gross violation of hospitality etiquette—and feels for thin reverberations to come through the thick black plastic, which soon arrive given the young woman's propensity for her voice to travel longitudinally, screechingly, but not bracingly.

You and I are hardly surprised that Blanchot will not find the young woman in there. In fact, he does not want to open the bag. He relaxes his grip on its edge and feels reassured about everything, existence, the body, all and all and all. He has confirmed the falsity of body bag through etiquette—hence, the young woman's body—and the falsity of every body bag, giving poor shape to shapelessness, providing false contours, false outlines of the subject it holds, its opaque, dull drudgery. For a few consecutive nights, I have him visit the body bag in this way as the incarnation of the American ur-friend, and he observes himself communicating with it in a language he does not identify—a strange development because he always speaks in French in his dreams, a much better French than you and I have spoken in ours, but this being a French spoken as if it were prelapsarian.

He pulls back. Observing a gentle woman who was never a gentle woman aside, towards the back of the room, he nods to her in universal greeting. She, however, does not respond. She never responds, other than smoking a cigarette diligently, calmly, but not respectfully, holding in the same hand a white ceramic coffee cup where the faint outline of blood gathers around the edge of her thumb pressing against its side.

The balcony overlooks the sidewalks of an aberrant, self-loathing city he no longer recognizes while she grasps the strange wrought-iron patterns as though for whatever dear life she has, leaving the coffee cup on his desk, herself also leaving in a pattern of thin televisional and radiological voices outside which, to him, is neither a comfort nor a reassurance of any pattern.

Because the Hotel Chelsea for Maurice Blanchot cannot exist if not filled with ur-friends.

In a hotel, any hotel, every hotel, a guest is always being carried out when they are discovered, and everyone always wants to be discovered at the Hotel Chelsea. It construes the very antithesis of an actual hotel since staying at a hotel is the antithesis of being almost famous, always being insistent even when his or her presence is shielded to all besides the lonely perverts who wander the hallways late night, some looking for Jesus to enter their heart, some decidedly not, who place their hands on the succession of wooden doors, imagining who may be residing behind them and what they may be doing with their meanwhile with the gentle men and gentle women who no longer wish to be gentle in rooms where wishes are easily granted.

In the midst of occasional not-writing when he is done reading the lobby newspapers or commiserating with the almost famous guests who chat him up on the hotel's other almost famous guests who are not his immediate concern, in the suspension of every wish of his own, Maurice Blanchot becomes the loneliest pervert not looking for Jesus at the Hotel Chelsea to speak prelapsarian French. He sees the hypothetical manuscript he attempts must plumb the depths for new ur-friends in his life, must follow the anonymous bloody thumb-print down the hallway, so that the knowledge may lead to a gentle woman who is no longer a gentle woman who does not occupy a body bag. His walk is calm, assured, particularly for one who understands there is no other scent to cover his fine Parisian smell, no dampening carpet in the hallways to muffle his steps and the possibility of almost famous guests he may run into happenstance out in the hallway and who tell him impromptu fragments laced with profane smoke and unfamiliar smells, all the while doing his best not to cough out loud.

In Room 331, he relinquishes the possibility of knowing who resides on this floor with him. There is only the sifting elsewhere. Room 219. Room 407. Various rooms, various floors guests pass through—no, he corrects himself, are *allowed* to pass through. Room 1108. Room 644. Invited, uninvited. Room 519. All guests granted passage but never going in or out. Room 100. Consumed. Sorted. Dispersed. Himself.

The young man in the black leather jacket, the gentle man who was never a gentle man, is a building where there is no lobby, no coffee, no paintings, no almost famous guests, no room. Except himself.

Putting down a copy of Marguerite Duras currently occupying his attention, Blanchot gets up from a deeply wounded upholstered chair and wanders over to the balcony doors in his room, opens them. He offers the rain his inspection, measuring its quality, volume, consistency, acidic composition, other intangibles. It is not the soft Parisian rain of aquatints but a leadened sort which proves somewhat overbearing to him, the constant want for company that it brings.

Who are his neighbors, he speculates.

Who are neighbors, he asks.

The problem with cockroaches. He wants to like them. For awhile, distracted watching them at a distance in his room, he thinks he does. It piques him how adept they are at knowing when they have been made out, how the suspension of their movements as calculations are made as to their next course of action, their quickest route of escape, and yet they will never make that move until set upon with a shoe or rolled-up newspaper. If not for this evolutionary shortcoming, he muses, cockroaches could have become the masters of us all, provided they are not already. A minor proof of this arrives: a little guest brave enough to make its claim to his typed manuscript pile sits there, antennas pointing at Blanchot. Peculiar specimen. Instinctively grabbing the white ceramic coffee cup with the bloody thumb-print and inverting it, he traps the cockroach underneath. Now what will I do with it, he thinks, or what was I planning to do with it if not to have it suffer entrapment. The moment is not lost on him. He does believe, as he goes to sleep that same night, leaving the cup as it is, the little guest is suffering somehow, a suffering not attenuated to loss or even stasis, but being separated from the knowledge of it being discovered, being found by another, for which it must now wait, starve, reconsider, and completely rely on its own conclusions about not only what is happening but what is *here* as well, what is *now*.

To walk into a building where, as he is told by the Chelsea's almost famous guests, gentle men who were never gentle men are being detained and questioned,

   which means he will be willing if not able to tell the people there is information regarding a gentle woman who was never a gentle woman killed, whom he has had a chance to depose indirectly, that he has made a connection with her and discovered her bloody thumb-print on a coffee cup, which likely has nothing to do with the circumstances of her death, though perhaps this bit of information, true or not true, helpful or not helpful, could provide clarification to this murder of some cultural importance which renders a gentle man who is no longer a gentle man as an almost famous guest at this building;

   which means he is not entirely certain why he wants to walk into this building or what he hopes to accomplish for himself if not a gentle man who was never a gentle man who does not deserve his help, intercession or mere company, and maybe he will do this for the sake of entering a strange building that tells him he has no business entering, something akin to a Hotel Chelsea with a security checkpoint, video cameras he has never seen before endlessly scanning and recording, all of which announce the withholding of expecting comfort, privacy, civility, and cultural import;

   which means he enters this building so he may expect the worst in of itself, and let itself be recognized by him, because walking into a building where the worst in of itself may reside means there is hesitation, disbelief, the blank stares at a faulty attempt of non-prelapsarian language so someone at the front desk may grant him access, of what his own scent in this building will be and to realize his mistake of showering before going there and offending the neutral air with a fine Parisian lather;

which means he should not waste the building's Time so willingly, the person at the front desk will tell him, since: (a) wanting information from the building is a clear breach of protocol, (b) wanting information from the gentle man who was never a gentle man is a clear breach of protocol, or (c) saying anything to help a gentle woman who was never a gentle woman, who cannot be helped anymore in any way, who does not reside in this building, is clear breach of protocol;

which means walking out of a building he never actually enters does not mean leaving it;

which means walking around several blocks of urban blight to purge external dialogue from his thoughts (he thinks this is an insufficient narrative element anyway);

which means he should have checked into a hotel where nothing appears to happen but everything does happen, and have been writing in a room where there is no building to speak of but the room itself.

A gentle woman holds the door open at the Chelsea for a gentle man who may no longer be a gentle man. He says nothing to her, having refused to shower for several days.

Returning directly to the typewriter in his room, like all good writers he admires, he is unable to write anything.

As a gentle man who may no longer be a gentle man wanders the hallways of the hotel at night, knowing the scents, knowing all the not so famous guests are sleeping and the almost famous guests think they are sleeping, you want me to lead him out of the building, lead him to the understanding that guests cannot be helped for walking into a building they cannot leave, because you, having never visited the Hotel Chelsea, service the rooms for only one guest. Because you and you all keep failing to realize the Chelsea is not any kind of a hotel. A hotel filled with little guests in their insect captivity. Unlikely. Inescapable. The faint knife of a deleterious existence with routine check-outs and the occasional stray word in the lobby, an unwashed coffee cup, and of waiting, waiting, rapprochement with the other in the room, always another guest, sleeping, typing out notes, no room service, no room without you and me, his neighbors of the everlasting.

Someone in a room on the third floor overheard something else someone in another room said impolite, shouted through the door and radiating out into the hallway, filled with recrimination and obscenity almost comedic, which you and I know from our hallway excursions strangely happens when a din is raised, but this is not the comedy which enters a work of cultural importance at any given moment.

Another guest wakes up, non-plussed, trying to jiggle his nightstand lamp to function, without success.

On his desk, blocked by an inverted coffee cup, a manuscript he has stopped working on. Throwing himself out of bed, neglecting his slippers, he angles himself in the dark toward it. On the first page he finds his little guest still alive (such a slight survivor of that *here* and *now*) who promptly scurries off as he raises and smashes the coffee cup on the floor, leaving a jagged piece with an anonymous bloody thumb-print intact.

The abrupt coldness of the floor he treads tightens off the blood in his toes. He wraps the piece in a kerchief and places it in his luggage. He notices the shouts have stopped now, yet there remain footsteps which sound in the hallway outside his door, their approaching filling the quiet of his room, and another scent he recognizes.

Maurice Blanchot says the room of Maurice Blanchot is where you and I must bring an end to a room, any room, every room.

*

There will be a morning where you and I may gather the pages that, we have been told, Maurice Blanchot wrote for his unpublished novel, provided to us by our upstairs neighbor, attempted at the famous Hotel Chelsea with a manual typewriter, the thinning, pressed script of a language against a mere vapor of paper-stock barely registering beyond my looking past a coffee cup I drink from.

You may tell her, then, after my story, you do not believe Blanchot wrote this shitty, pointless novel.

At first you will struggle translating the peculiar French translated into less peculiar English while our upstairs neighbor looks on, smiling at us in a way which smiles are unreadable, and remark how the words barely convey their subject.

You understand well enough there is at least something resembling a story that resembles a day.

The day is set in a hotel. Later, it is discovered not to be a hotel. Interiority abounds. What little action there is set at a hotel that is not really a hotel revolves around a gentle man who is no longer a gentle man and a gentle woman who is no longer a gentle woman who could be his most gentle lover, albeit in the strangest possible way, along with a third party of indeterminate origin, an interloper whose connection to the other two principal characters is undefined, the triangle unmistakable.

So that their story may be told over and over to future guests, the interloper wants to take both of their thumb-prints in blood, convinced that this documentation is the only way to rebuild the hotel into an actual hotel, which you have significant reservations about since the narrator has the interloper transgress all normal expectations of how a hotel operates. Regardless, the actual hotel will remain thanks to the documentation. The other guests who are not gentle will all become gentle again. The face of the interloper, if you squint at the language on the pages long enough, if you had repeatedly watched *Sid and Nancy* with your famous sister, if you want to believe the dreams you had in tandem with your famous sister about the afterlife reunion, will resemble a young Gary Oldman in his prime.

You won't say any of this to our upstairs neighbor. You want to tell her instead that you do not believe she wrote this manuscript, either.

She likely finishes folding her laundry without a rejoinder, still smiling.

Waiting for our collaborative delicates to finish drying, you and I will watch her depart the laundry room in an impolite turn of yellowish white hair. Her long, abortive sigh left is behind for our usual edification which, with lavender or lilacs, April and May, follows her out into the hallway, and away to another apartment, another room upstairs only seen for ourselves in what is certain to be an unpublished novel.

You must secretly fear that novel for the sake of those who will no longer visit us at night.

THE DISAPPOINTMENT OF MAURICE BLANCHOT VISITING NIAGARA FALLS

SOMEONE—A SUPER, and not so—threatens us with water. Or not. Or the lack of it. For an unpaid bill, for unpaid rent, for unpaid taxes, for a broken water pipe needing repair, for contamination or imitation. Always some reason multiplying. A reason of some needing some, some algorithm of a building's desire to remain a building with tenants inside. A reason to threaten tenants who need water for coffee or hot baths or laundry, as though these were luxuries, and they are, someone, a super, very much so, says to us in a notice, a brochure, some letter or not. Someone writes something—in this case, about water—and a whole building pays attention. Or you and I do. Tenants who need water. Others, only to be reminded of some water. So much water. So few working pipes, hey. A tenant can never appreciate these things living in a single building long enough says super and not so. Origin. Access. Delivery. Arrival. The threat of all these, or none of these. The abundance or absence or both. Having to watch it over and over and again. A scene, appreciating us, forever inside it, while coffee is made, hot baths are drawn and laundry is done, as if by themselves. Someone's desire. Finally, and not so.

*

It is after your chance encounters with our upstairs neighbor in the basement, you doing load upon load of laundry, hoping that we still have water, that you often ask me, Why do you always write like you're writing for Gary Oldman,

as if I have had any choice in the matter given my tenuous relationship with you and your famous sister, as well as Gary Oldman's tenuous relationship with a world seething with violent alcoholic impulses which gentle people could never divorce themselves from, no matter how many *Sid and Nancy* viewings they take in with those who are closest to them on the sofa, and touching,

Which kinda feels like eternity, I imagine you grumble to the immutable soul of your famous sister when I am not around, though I am around, here, sitting on an unused washing machine.

I mean, like, Gary Oldman, you say again to punctuate your question. You become more agitated with me while I keep sitting, and you fold our laundry with no small dexterity into neat little piles growing less smaller. Seriously, we're just barely getting by this month and my sister and, like, Gary Fucking Oldman you—

as our upstairs neighbor possessing thirteen unpublished manuscripts returns to separate the lights from the darks from the dryer as one would separate lavender from lilacs, April from May, all in the vain attempt to diffuse your blatant profanity common in the aberrant, self-loathing city that, no doubt, she would rather not be a part of in this laundry room while in the midst of thinking about Maurice Blanchot's perfumed white body. She turns off the lights as she enters, the only light coming in from barred windows high and close to the ceiling. Despite the machines in the basement humming and churning around all three us in the dark, you do not seem to mind that she will hear how Los Angeles has not contacted me yet about Gary Oldman and the latest personal technology he will be vouching for and how I should be the one to put the words into his mouth instead of, perhaps, your famous sister outside the Gehry Museum when she met him after trying to walk through a plate-glass door

failing to push aside the dramatic persona, leaving the here and now of Gary Oldman for the gentle woman who has written twelve novels but never published any of them to behold, one that is innately tied to my memories of you and your famous sister wandering the American cultural topography of a worn-down VHS copy of *Sid and Nancy* and only finding it a Möbius strip extending out and further as it attempts the cosmic balancing act of a failed etiquette revealed. I would like to tell you, if I write about this Gary Oldman long enough, that the Möbius strip will finally reveal itself to us, or we will find a way to break it forever and release ourselves to the true afterlife reunion where your famous sister awaits us—or you await me, at least. I tell you the I writes like I am writing for Gary Oldman so I do not have to write any further about the gentle man who is no longer a gentle man who may have already achieved his afterlife reunion, albeit on a much different astral plane than Gary Oldman as Sid Vicious (or not so different), and who will never see if the Gehry Museum exists in Los Angeles outside the mind of Gary Oldman, much to the detriment of his true understanding of architecture and my understanding of literature. Somewhere out there, I attest, is the last great hope of my own that the Gehry Museum which exists only in the mind of Gary Oldman is the building we will never want to leave—not for its beauty, its truth, its labyrinthine etiquette trapping us and holding us, but because, like the gentle man who is no longer a gentle man, our recognition of a building is something we will never leave is implicit. So why not reside in that world of cold beauty overseen by the administrator of din, and chat with those who reside with us and converse forever in the anecdotal to help pass eternity while entrapped in the ice. There may be art there. Art, when bearable, can always be entertaining or edifying or both. Like little gobsmacked children we will happily push—and only push—open the plate-glass doors, pay our admission fee, Abandon Hope, and reside in this world with the other subjugated beings begging to catch a scrap of relief from the former buildings they once inhabited, crying out to you and you all, Let me tell you, and, I was once alive, and, Tell others of me

in the dark smiling dry smiles, she adds.

Perhaps to no one's surprise, especially yours, the sadness of the gentle woman who has written twelve novels but never published any of them knows almost ten thousand stories of Niagara Falls as the *de facto* suicide vacation capital of North America, which she references as would an imaginary counterfeit of a brochure to be handed out free of charge to novices of the eternal.

Since she has only one such experience—what you would call in your profession the *idealization of suicide*—or very limited imagination to draw upon for herself these things, the most she can do is tell you and me over our still-churning lights and darks of the intersection of her life with this beauty which was indeed the escape she dared not speak of, lest her raised voice violated all that could be considered polite and kind. A world Maurice Blanchot would see as falling around us in the variegated breaking of water down to its smallest parts without ever ceasing to be water and becoming its mere molecular components instead, a world, perhaps, not much different than the Hotel Chelsea, Mann's Chinese Theater, or even the laundry room in this basement despite his latent hydrophobia surfacing around when they first met, underscored by his lack of personal hygiene at the commencement of their professional working relationship.

It is true, our upstairs neighbor concedes, Blanchot did not write extensively about the healing feminine symbolism of water or even about Nature in general, if only because, she thinks, he was far too concerned with buildings and hierarchy and waiting and the eternal to be overly impressed with large amounts of an abundant natural resource we take for granted here in America but perhaps not so much in Paris. A good enough reason to dream of it, I respond, and upon saying this, the dream of saying occurs finally to the Maurice Blanchot who belongs to the sadness of this gentle woman, for him to discover what is not there in front of him inside him, like any writer of unpublished novels, sending him from his bed (if it is indeed his bed), playing the Chang Chou and the Butterfly game with himself upon turning the knob on his bedroom door that he senses his own turning sending him to the side, on a pivot as it were, understanding he would not go anywhere until he woke up from being a doorknob, which meant, of course, leaving the building for good, his building, the Hotel Chelsea he thought he would never leave, until now

adjourning to the bathroom to reluctantly throw water on his dirty face and help accelerate this waking-up, he finds something horrendous about water—lots of it, altogether. The rush, the swell, the formlessness. Waves. No waves. Tidepools. Stagnation. Bulbous kelp. Dreary crustaceans. Gulls hovering everywhere, shitting on gentle people trying to enjoy water. He feels nothing for the sea. Anything of abundance, regardless of how it is channeled, whether by cruelty, etiquette or porcelain coffee cups, strikes no fear into him (for, really, he thinks, there is indeed nothing to fear whatsoever), but the thought of being overwhelmed by his sight sends a certain death brushing against his sleeve, not unlike being asphyxiated by a single green pea lodged in the windpipe, or having a penny dropped on his head after being tossed from the rooftop of a very tall building. Drowning in a large pool of water, not so much

unless, he reconsiders, reconnecting the phone jack in his room that he had been dreaming about to call a yellow taxi, he could view himself in the moment of his drowning, surrounded by people of all gentle persuasions watching and somehow approving of this spectacle by their watching inofitself, even if they weren't pointing and laughing at him while it happened, and they likely would not be unless outside of all buildings a failed etiquette was afoot.

Maurice Blanchot has been unaware, as is herself, as are most gentle people in general who are not sad, exactly how many gentle people over the years have killed themselves at Niagara Falls by tossing their bodies over the precipice or have committed accidental suicide because of going over in a barrel or a more modern barrel-like apparatus resembling a large insulated egg more than an actual barrel. Writer that he is, he is fairly certain an old story must loom behind the public phenomena all the same, some narrative which exists only to forever link the Falls to death itself or the nature of death, and the gathering crowd around it to death-as-spectacle, alleviated from the abundance of water viewed in a sense of awe and majesty, and ten thousand cheap delights clustered around it. The gentle woman knows the story: another legend, another young woman, whose sway over the locals has allowed her to draw her necromantic caresses over many an unfortunate immutable soul ready to leave this world, afterlife reunion or no. In fact, she says, she has studied it very well. Well enough to try writing a manuscript about her (and you are not the least bit surprised about this) in the vein of Maurice Blanchot. In the throes of such whiteness, then, our upstairs neighbor made many a trip to sit at one of the benches parked beside the Falls to consider eradication—namely her own— and not have to face the shame of returning to her unpublished novels for the meandering professor to eventually read or a hairless agent to reject. It's funny, she had realized, how the Falls would provoke such shame in her by providing the means to avoid it, watching the endless, cascading stream of violent water go over the edge and thinking, That could be me, because such thoughts come easily to those who are gentle in every conceivable way, especially when they know they will never be published or be read by anyone who is anything other than gentle.

As our upstairs neighbor reiterates, Blanchot was not the kind of gentle man who feels shame so easily, if at all, but did feel the otherworldly presence of absence as acutely as any Gary Oldman would. Perhaps it would be better, then, if I had Maurice Blanchot and Gary Oldman meeting somehow, somewhere, if not in Niagara Falls, discussing literature despite the significant discrepancy of age and educational background and contrasting disciplines (Gary Oldman could never stay as still as Maurice Blanchot would have at the Hotel Chelsea unless he was indeed Sid Vicious), but, no, these two can never meet any more than Gehry Museum can exist in Los Angeles in the mind of Gary Oldman. Such chance encounters can only be an aberration, which Gary Oldman will avoid after his own with your famous sister, not wanting to sign a stranger's life away again. It is easier seeing Blanchot with the gentle woman, even if I do not have to believe her.

Maurice Blanchot making his first visit to Niagara Falls means anything other than the picaresque Niagara Falls all gentle people know and love passively, quickly, but not intensely.

He must view it in a rainy downpour, with no tourists around him, cold damp and grey dreary, a dreariness already paid to the administrator of din as he withholds the scrap of porcelain he has kept in his pocket as a receipt of his stay at the Hotel Chelsea before arriving here. This is quite fitting, he thinks, having come this far to take solace in nature for once, in what mankind could never provide for itself (assuming, of course, the Maurice Blanchot I narrate believes in mankind), and find himself utterly abandoned, with the excepting privilege of Madame Tussaud's Wax Museum behind him on the hill where famous company always awaits (with the exception of Gary Oldman since the cultural significance of *Sid and Nancy* has yet to be revealed to the world) and finding instead the quintessence reduced to running water falling from a very great height.

Not nearly as impressive as Victoria Falls in Africa, he mulls, but that is the point: why stand in awe of the world when the downfall of gentle men and gentle women who are no longer gentle await.

Fetching the porcelain scrap from his pocket, Blanchot tosses it into the spiraling tidal pool below which he cannot see, as though it were a gigantic wishing well, knowing that soon the bloody thumb-print will be erased, the porcelain scrap reduced to a mere pebble smoothness over Time and join its brethren in uniformity on the floor.

Unlike the porcelain scrap, Maurice Blanchot is a gentle man who does not need millions of gallons of water at a single moment to reduce him to smoothness, sighs the sadness of our upstairs neighbor. She is folding bedsheets that, to the trained eye, have the appearance of being filched from the Hotel Chelsea, and thus have no need to ever leave her laundry hamper. But, she adds, since he has stopped taking showers at this point during his American sojourn, a world of architecture made by water now seems slightly more frightening to him, more so since he has never considered suicide by drowning before, but the great Niagara Falls, one of the wonders of the world, and here he is, having been dismayed by the aberrant, self-loathing city that ruined his hypothetical manuscript, a novel of fleeting, intelligent prose that could be the best ur-friend its readers ever had, if only one reader found it and not all the others who would pick up his manuscript and hate it because they had never stayed at the Hotel Chelsea, never searched out Niagara Falls as the final gesture of a failed etiquette.

Staring at the Falls from the Canadian side, Maurice Blanchot becomes interested in the roaring, falling water signing a life away, and that somewhere, in once such crescendo, is the signature which will end his life, grant him an everlasting fame which he has never sought nor even found attractive. It is a signature which would explain many things to him, writ large by the unseen hand dooming his gentle body no longer smelling of Parisian lather to a building of unimaginable depths, leaving him to rot forever there as you and I roam over him, asking him questions, while those outside gaze at the magnificence of the truth beauty of falling water while neglecting its siren song, all these cheap distractions part of the design to avoid this building which never sends us forth but keeps the gentle body in a torment ranging from Forever to Something Resembling Forever—like ice, for instance. Is this what the young woman felt, Blanchot thinks. A visitor at a hotel she soon knew she would never leave because the price of waiting to leave the building could never be paid, signed away in one last gentle act to redeem herself, to have you and I walk among the faces until our feet touch the ice, and return her to the world outside, which, I should say, is no world. Only an aberration. A mere anecdote.

You're not supposed to litter the water, a voice next to Blanchot says, they're one of the world's seven wonders—plus this isn't the States, you know.

He turns. There is a disheveled young woman wearing what appears to be a large plastic garbage bag as a raincoat beside him.

Water should be plural *waters* here, he may say to her.

Just paying my admission fee, he responds instead. Facetious. Very unlike him.

There's no fee, she replies testily. The Falls are free to the world, of course. As they should be. Forever.

Of course.

Also—people have died here. Many good people. Show some respect, please.

Ah.

His Ah, our upstairs neighbor explains further to you and me, is meant to have the Parisian effect of conveying to her how he was somewhat annoyed to be lectured about respect and have his solitude broken or to have been caught in what this person may believe to be a desecration, a concept which he is not entirely familiar with since he likely believes everything in the world is already desecrated for being in it, perhaps following some latent Buddhist impulse, following further still what to do with a woman who is obviously trying to get his attention by making him feel somewhat stupid or indelicate—a new feeling for him. He is not at all accustomed to being trapped, especially by people wearing trash bags as raincoats as though they have lived their whole lives on the streets, which he has decidedly not. Recognizing this makes him feel sorry that he threw the porcelain chip into the water, and he debates whether to jump in after it, to both retrieve it and put an end to his life simultaneously in front of her, to have him leave her. Or her leaving him. Whichever comes first.

This would be a fair way to die, Blanchot wants to explain to her, and would you care to join me, knowing full well no one will see anything, and leave them in the whirlpool for days before anyone realized anything was wrong, before sending them into the gorge to be found by a tourist boat. A somewhat unfitting end for himself, he reconsiders, but it could be perfect for her.

The bloody thumb-print weighs heavy in Blanchot's considerations.

He senses he has made a mistake, as though it were the last signature of a gentle woman who was never a gentle woman who did not deserve to die because she was never a gentle woman with her own signature, special, eternal, but not liminal to the last viewer who could come to Niagara Falls and, surpassing Madame Tussaud's, find your famous sister waiting in a building with no doors except for one, a plate-glass door that one must walk through if the eternal is to be braved, if the eternal can ever be braved, that is, knowing that for every Virgil who knows Hell well enough to be a tour guide there must be a Dante who occasionally forsakes Heaven as a narrator, regardless of how well it ends for him, that he comes through the darkness into the light, bearing tens of thousands of signatures in a book that are all the same bloody thumb-print on a mankind that cannot be reconciled anymore than the waters can at Niagara Falls.

I was nearly one, the young woman wearing a trash bag says unexpectedly to him, walking toward the metal railing as though anticipating his thoughts, his impulses, the failed cultural dialectic of an America he has emerged from to take refuge in the mental architecture of nature, far far away from the aberrant city, and why not, she enjoins him, take my hand and let us leave the phoniness of Madame Tussaud's behind for the afterlife reunion you and I were meant to have, star-crossed as we are, unfortunate as we'll always be—

Yes, interrupts Blanchot, I know, I have been—he starts, not sure how to explain why he was carrying a porcelain scrap with a bloody anonymous thumb-print on it or why he is here when he is supposed to be in Paris writing not for the whims of myself trying to discover the origins of a manuscript which should have never been, swallowed by the own tempestuous waters of a failed etiquette which cannot be resolved but only left behind as one may leave a building should the choice be apparent.

And he stares at Niagara Falls in the cold, grey rain with a gentle woman who may not be gentle, though, choice of attire aside, she would seem to know a few things about the human impulse towards the spectacle of death and the following abundance, as she takes his hand, noting blood on it— a cut, it appears, from the porcelain shard that he had somehow missed. He feels the depth of the cut as the gentle woman fishes out a kerchief from her pocket and tightly binds it to staunch the wound as he lets out a demure, Ouch, the deed quickly done and her holding the bandaged hand up to him, as if saying, I did this for you and it wasn't half bad.

You are good with your hands, he tells her politely, graciously, but not frivolously.

She looks at him.

You should read my manuscripts, then, before we throw ourselves in.

Sidling up beside her, he takes her hand with his bandaged one, this strange woman who makes little sense to him, a woman he may have seen before elsewhere, in some mental state, in some absence he filled with the memory of those who left him without so much as a letter goodbye, a final cup of coffee. There, looking out onto the cascading water with her, he senses it was never his own insignificance at stake but every impulse leading over the metal railing which he never took until now, with this woman wearing a trash bag who tells him she has been writing novels, and standing at this hollowed edge of where every gentle man and gentle woman visits but never understands, the siren song never heard, knowing he had already lost his life to this gentle woman who has always been gentle.

It is here, smiling the driest of smiles in the dark, he must ask her what I cannot: Why do you want to write like you are writing for me.

Because, she will say much later, I have never visited Niagara Falls again since that day. The day the disappointment of you visiting Niagara Falls was cured in my modest room at the Rainbow Dreams Motel by virtue of the first shower you had taken in months. The day for always remembering what your body smells like fresh from Parisian lather coming out of that shower. The day you read every single one of my twelve novels I carried in two briefcases which were to go into the waters with me. The day you gave me possession of your last unpublished manuscript before returning to Paris to never write again. The day I decided to never write again. For you. The day you and I realized there was no further suffering to inflict upon ourselves by returning to Niagara Falls

her turning with basket of dried and folded lights and darks in hand,

The day that all I had in a day: the bar of soap you traveled with.

*

When it is late at night again, you and I travel down our hallway with deep-bottomed plastic receptacles in hand, looking for any available water since the super has followed through on his threat and turned all of it off in the building for some reason, with a predictably curt notice on our door indicating some reason. You are angry. Being without water is somehow my fault, connected to my waiting for Gary Oldman. Why couldn't you be more like Maurice Blanchot, I hear you complain about me. But I do not respond. The reason for being without water is not as interesting as the search for water itself. It is a fine way to meet ur-friends, not to become Maurice Blanchot.

You and I are re-enacting an old story, perhaps the oldest of them all, perhaps the beginning of all narrative, I say instead, as you ignore my wondering out loud blithely, aimlessly, but not purposefully what your famous sister would have done without water since I imagine being told by someone in a building that she was not bathing in her final days with the gentle man who is no longer a gentle man, which left her skin in something of a molting and scabrous state while his remained remarkably smooth to the touch, or to the touch of roughened hands, those not accustomed to water other than a drain, especially a drain's insides, where the custom of accumulation slurs your famous sister down to where the repository awaits our waiting, our waiting forever, sitting, in a building of water you and I wander to consult the anecdotal progeny of faceless deeds in the aberrant, self-loathing city, below, asking us, Why this slurred water when there was none for us, to which you and I must wait first for the incessant lips to end their moving. You and I consider their words reaching us, looking past door after door, your hand tugging at mine, surprisingly eager to look upon these faces, these bodies not enough to touch the ice ever, the faculties of living in this slurred water when once none was to be had has now been ruination to their best sense of that world you and I continue to wander, which they ask about—especially novels. They all want to know about novels more than anything. They no longer care about the state of gentle people, their current lives, their pleasures, their governments, who won the biggest games, who bagged the most desirable spouse. Gary Oldman, I confess, was also not at the forefront of their concerns. I consider explaining that they should be more concerned about Gary Oldman given their eternal predicament. His example may be more helpful to them in that regard.

Yet they insist upon the novels, something they are not allowed to have here. The current brings the other transubstantiated debris though skittering fingers until they watch it dissipate, merge fully with the slurred water itself and disappear from sight, while those more observant weep for the shame, the indignation upon realizing they have nothing further to contribute to any narrative because of the indisputable fact of their weeping before us, as you and I, always practical in our exorbitant cohabitation scheme, begin collecting their tears for our morning coffee.

BLACK BOY READS
(FOREVER) HIMSELF

SOMETIMES I THINK I would follow you everywhere I could if, that is, I do not follow you everywhere now in some sense. Follow you assuredly like the black boy follows you at the social building where his curses reverberate in the hallways so everyone there can hear his epithets directed towards a certain part of your anatomy. Except, of course, I would not curse you in such a way despite having better knowledge than the black boy insofar as he has yet to understand his role in the afterlife reunion to help summon and ferry those across to another place where there is no day and no building and no social workers and no rec room and no place that he fulfills with his presence. Getting him there with the others, I contend, won't be so easy. Nothing with the black boy ever is. If I follow you to the social building under the pretense of some thin perversion playing itself out in front of your co-workers, perhaps I could help resolve your dilemma by making him understand Gary Oldman better, which will make him understand himself better, as it makes all of us understand ourselves better, that we are gentle people and not really so horrible, not like whatever incarnation Gary Oldman presents to us when he is not sight-seeing in Los Angeles and considering whether the Gehry Museum really exists or not.

Finishing your coffee, you defer on my suggestion with any number of digressions on hand to draw attention to my foolishness. We've got, like, enough problems, you say in so many words, and they all can't be readily solved by the example of Gary Oldman. Literature may be more helpful. But I'm sure Gary Oldman reads constantly, I protest, but you deposit your coffee cup in our desertbone dry sink and head off to the bedroom to change for work, neglecting the potential of Gary Oldman's literacy for that of the black boy's, and what, if anything, he would read with as much diligence as his cursing you.

If only Maurice Blanchot cursed more in his work, I prefer having you think, or had I allowed him to curse aloud in French-inflected English, maybe the black boy would be more interested in what the manuscript would have to say to him, unlike the ones which speak of beauty truth or double consciousness or the inner workings of a chrysalis of language pushing the subject out of its own and, hence, culture. But there is no culture of cursing for the black boy beyond that of a Gary Oldman in Los Angeles ready to shoot a commercial for the latest personal technology that Maurice Blanchot would abhor, any Maurice Blanchot I could think of. Then you consider whether I could narrate a curse for the black boy, the best thing I could do for him, no craft hour, no soup line, no redirection, no rec room, no social building, no building at all. Because a curse is the opposite of a building. An anti-building. An ur-building. Everything built upon, yet nothing there. A vacuation or vacation or both without the you. A place the black boy would love to be, if only could leave his lips.

What is difficult about a curse that Blanchot could fail at. Why can't you just give the black boy the manuscript. How could he read it. What's the point of his reading. Why do you think he thinks about reading. Anything with a why. Because that's where. That's why. You'll never know when, either. It's a failure, not a curse. You can't walk into a failure, but you can always walk into a plate-glass door. Which is a curse. Blanchot could walk through it, depending on how he walks when you walk, down to the subway, up to the wayway, cross the street and there to your building, what it is when you are why. Why am I here, you ask no one, especially yourself. The black boy. Because that's a where. That's not a why, however. Closer to a curse. A curse interrupted by his curse, or the memory of his smell as he sat less than five feet away from you in your shabby cubicle. Better than the curse or smell of Gary Oldman even and any of his wheres which don't include your famous sister. Yet you want to include her. Even famous, she is still your sister, not a bloody thumb-print. Not a sidewalk no one walks upon because they are too busy cursing.

Such cursing is easier with a hypothetical unpublished translated novel by Blanchot in your satchel waiting to be read by someone who does not follow you everywhere. Would that be the black boy. Anything can happen on a train. All destinies cross somewhere, but only by an accident, an aberration, a self-loathing. Black boys running after a taxi cab with Sid Vicious and Nancy Spungen in the afterlife reunion. My drowning in the steam of hot water by your hand, if we had any. The cursory glance. Someone cursing loudly in the seat behind you. The seventh son of a seventh son in the seat in front. None of that matters to the building you're about to enter, not even anecdotally. Why fake it. Why chase after it. There is no one in there. There is no one driving. There is no one to hold the door open for you.

You begin dreaming at night of the black boy walking through a plate-glass door, then interrogating the dream's ill intent while at work, the malice of either you failing to help him or pushing him through the door, both of which you desire.

A scene of the black boy reading a hypothetical unpublished translated novel by Maurice Blanchot in an abandoned building in the aberrant, self-loathing city would seem absurd to you for any number of reasons, even if I may remind you that you have to be the one who gives the black boy the manuscript when he does not likely know what a manuscript is, much less a manual typewriter, but you think this would play itself out like the end of *Sid and Nancy*, of Gary Oldman as Sid Vicious eating a slice of pizza and waiting for the afterlife reunion with Chloe Webb as three black boys serenade him with the boombox playing disco and he dances his dance in self-deprecation while the black boys totally eat it up and egg him on, the whiteness of Sid Vicious as Gary Oldman becoming so painfully apparent that you hold on for dear life until the taxi rolls up with the corresponding whiteness of Nancy to whisk him away from the embarrassment of his life and the black boys run after him like a trail of streamers and cans attached to the back of a wedding limo, leaving them all behind.

Your black boy would be the one to get it. Your black boy would the one to stop chasing that taxi speeding away into the afterlife reunion with two gentle people who were never gentle to begin with and dedicate himself to the higher purpose among the ruins of a failed etiquette they had walked among and called home without really saying anything to the effect. How could he be the least important person in your life.

In Time, the sublimated delights of Gary Oldman feed the world of children until they are no longer children. This is not to say, however, they reach adulthood.

The black boy has never cared much for the sublimated delights of Gary Oldman for reasons that have less to do with the fact the black boy is black and more to do with the whiteness of Gary Oldman himself. This whiteness is not far removed from the whiteness of, for instance, a famous literary white whale, that perhaps Gary Oldman's best literary ur-friend is an atheist as Blanchot would have no doubt speculated upon had he been writing this instead of myself, a turn which throws the black boy for the proverbial loop in his dead mother's kitchen as he peers behind a piece of tattered fabric, looking for a can of soup in a hopeless pantry before he runs off to find you, that anyone could believe there is no geedee. Otherwise, what's the point of cursing.

Since the black boy curses so well and lets out another when the soup can fails to materialize before him, jamming his hand all the way into the back of the dark pantry and behind the crumbling drywall-moistwall-wetwall where he can't see, chancing whatever unknown with rabid teeth may take its opportunity but he doesn't care because he's cursing loudly, almost loud enough for his dead mother to hear. The dead mother doesn't raise so much as an eyebrow off the sofa. He understands in the most perfect way there is no leaving this tenement building as Gary Oldman as Sid Vicious or as any other incarnation born of a violent alcoholic acting style which black boys like the black boy should really really enjoy but he can't because Gary Oldman's literary whiteness somehow interferes with the moment though he was kinda cool in *The Professional* in a disquieting way. The black boy has known men like that. Gentle men who are never gentle to begin with. Who are too white. The ones who would visit his dead mother before her deadness became an actuality writ large on her tiredness of the gentle men who are too white who came through her door, coming and leaving and sometimes trying to leave-come, a trick only a white man could think up, the dead mother once told her son when one such gentle man who is too white tried and left the building without much success. Sly cocksuckers, her dead speech meanders and worms through a haze of those clove cigarettes that made the black boy cough worse than her. He often gives up the possibility of conversation at any level knowing her deadness was soon approaching—the right occasion for making it out of there if he could find a can of soup for breakfast before he had to go off and meet you at the social building. Reaching all the way now into the back of pantry as far as his arm could stretch, he mutters every curse he had heard his dead mother use when the gentle man who is too white left and his leave-come made a benediction on the dead mother's thigh which he couldn't help to repeat in every flagrant obscenity possible, knowing her son knew them all too well at his age. Sometimes, even when he knew he could not find the soup can or knew it was never in there, he kept reaching, digging, splaying all his fingers out as though daring that something unknown to take a bite out of him, and this constituted the closest the black boy would ever arrive to Gary Oldman as Sid Vicious because you had to be a damn fool to walk through a plate-glass door but motherfuckin hungry to keep grabbing for a can of soup you knew was never there to begin with, especially for breakfast. It was not necessarily hunger but the reticence to see you, your change in disposition after what has happened to your famous sister, the change in your temperance at the office, slowly, surely, but not inconspicuously giving your personality a hardened edge of grimacing teeth and rolling eyes skyward for every co-worker making a shabby request, for every black boy who was not the black boy—a disposition suited for someone who smokes clove cigarettes the black boy noted to himself though he knew you did not, and would not, unless it were the last secret you would ever keep from everyone, like trying to drown me in the hot steam of our bathroom. That gave him the only measure of pride beyond rolling gentle men who are too white in the street, searching for the scent of cloves that marks them as having been with his dead mother, and then giving them a little extra for it. Just in case. He figures, too, he isn't the only black boy with a dead mother on the sofa out there. He's doing favors. Favors including the aggravation. One day it would be worth it for another black boy who wasn't himself.

That is what he tells you, at least.

He tells you in the darkening social building you have been working in all day because he won't let you leave while he has all this to tell, knowing it is your job to cater your listening to him. Meanwhile, your co-workers have scurried away because they are done listening for the day. They have listened to it all in ripeness or not. When you were particularly beaten down, you used to listen to it all with the deliberate posing sympathy of a strung-out Nancy Spungen nodding off, dreaming of bloody Sid with a surprise behind his back and a crooked grin. Most of the Time the only way you could survive your shifts at the social building after what happened to your famous sister was to stare down everyone and ask yourself, Wonder what's behind their back, ready for the last big surprise, you tell the black boy finally because you knows he will notice (if not fully comprehend) someday when you yourself follow your famous sister into breathless obscurity that all measure of fame and infamy and non-fame burnishes away in the last light of reasoning. Then there will be no curses, no breakfast soup, no Gary Oldman anymore, and all will be content and grave.

From your satchel you produce something the black boy has never seen before—much less heard about from the other black boys—a bundle of papers with writing on it done by, you explain, something called a *manual typewriter*. He shrugs. So fuckin what. Dumb bitch. But this Time you do not grimace your teeth or roll your eyes skyward. Instead, you explain reverently this is perhaps the unpublished final novel of a gentle man who is too white, given to you by an old woman who lives in the apartment above you and has never published a novel, and now you are giving him this novel to do with as he pleases because she herself can no longer do as she pleases with it.

The black boy does not understand why you are giving him the manuscript that could have been written by a gentle man who is too white for him. You do not understand, either, but such unilateral gestures are usually predicated upon acts of misunderstanding anyway, that no one can ever fully grasp the effect of a manuscript on any particular reader, so you send it off as a hope—a blind one at that—the black boy will make sense of it himself and will grant him knowledge, experience, sympathy for the Other, a new ur-friend, and a sense of his secure self in this uncertain world, this difficult Time. That may be asking for too much. You hope it is a combination of at least three of those boons, not just two or even one, which seems shallow to you as far as manuscripts go, that is, if Maurice Blanchot could be accused of writing a shallow manuscript, or Gary Oldman accused of giving a shallow performance—and I say no to the former, only the slightness of the man he plays, which then gleans forth the quality of quality which only a Gary Oldman could muster, and we all forgive him, assuredly, for having to take a mediocre role just to make ends meet (how often have I been there) or try his hand at a multi-million dollar remake of *Sid and Nancy*, much in the same way we could forgive Maurice Blanchot for writing a potentially mediocre manuscript about a Niagara Falls romance between a Frenchman and a failed writer. But the black boy is not prone to acts of forgiveness, especially where acts of creativity are concerned, as you have bore witness to during Craft Hour on monday-wednesday-fridays, watching him render to pieces the paper in front of him using the blunted drawing implement and spiraling it into a deeper and deeper gash until it reaches the surface of the table below, and even then he would not stop unless you grabbed him from behind and saved him from it.

This is who you are giving the manuscript to. You think about it one last Time. You hesitate. You reconsider. You cave. You tell him,

I'd like you to do with this as you please. I don't know who really wrote it. I didn't see anything. I don't know if it matters much who wrote it. If you really like it, you can keep it. If you want to. You can even say you wrote it later. Because I think you'll write it. It'll be your story. I just don't know if you'll want it.

The black boy regards this offer suspiciously, warily, but not lightly. Not for someone accustomed to receiving nothing from anyone in this fucked-up building, even if it is some shitty white people book he can't read anyway, but that's the *beauty*, he thinks, the word popping into his head on its own for the first Time in his short life, it's not a book, just whutchucallit, a man-you-skrip, passed to his hands and which can never be accounted for—not by you, at least—which only he owns, and no one else, understanding that you are also saying goodbye to him, for good, but that's cool, he's used to that, in fact, it comes to him quite easily

snatching it from you watching him run-run-running out

the darkening social building which stops no one running the last run as if he's just made the greatest heist of his life which his emptiness would betray the falsity of this accomplishment to the end of the street that doesn't end in a strict zoning sense though it actually does

when he knows even if he can't bring himself to admit it, but what else does he have but the forever of,

Hey too-white muthafuckas
watch me read your fuckin
man
you
skrip
before I burn. It. Up.

Except soon he is only gently waiting another Time in another derelict
tenement building once built for black people by white people, by the clearing
light of a full moon, something construed as natural light if any were to be
found in this vacant neighborhood coming through the windows in rough
apertures made by cast-aside bricks. They even put a tall chain-link fence with
razorwire around all this shit, too. Fools.

Finding an opening, the black boy tries his luck since he thinks it is
improving for a change. He takes a seat on the first dirty box he finds. It is very
quiet around him, he notices.

In his possession: a hypothetical unpublished translated novel by Maurice
Blanchot that he does not know could be by Maurice Blanchot or our upstairs
neighbor, even if neither is the case. Yet he remains curious because he is still
thinking of you. He uses a small damaged sterno container lit with a nudie
lighter he stole from a bodega though he does not smoke himself because of his
dead mother's clove cigarette habit. This seems a fortunate bit of manner since
he won't get any ashes on the manuscript. Whatever, I say he says. He doesn't
give two shits about what happens to it. He's not even sure why he is reading
it except for some misguided loyalty he feels for you now, picturing himself
abandoning you in your lame cubicle, how you tried to help quell the eternal
curse from his lips and generally turn his life around by having him read
things he couldn't possibly understand. Like possibly Blanchot.

From the first page on, the whiteness of Blanchot is an immediate turn-off,
daring the black boy to not draw his filthy dirty fuckin cursing hand across
the page and besmirch every thoughtful word with the accumulated hardness
of his aberrant, self-loathing life so that it is all re-written, every magnanimous
thought, every great humanistic impulse undone by the presence of he who

cannot appreciate a single word that is the polar opposite of a curse. But the black boy, being a black boy, has had to learn the simplest things last, which makes for difficulties. Significant ones, says the dead mother's smoke. To be sure, he has learned well from her untimely vapors there is something that does not love black boy, though he could think deep down good black boys would make good neighbors all the same without the chain-links should he go deep enough into the neighborhood, a brick in his hand. Other days, much that is black boy must be discarded by them, however, so that he may resemble a taller impression of himself upon returning home when he's done thinking he's done reading Maurice Blanchot and being confused. All because black boy, friends, is bore-reen, and he thinks hard for us all—his only swerving until memory believes before black boy remembers, before he says, I am black boy, I contain multitudes with my fuckin attitudes. A rosy-fingered black boy might have also shone upon their tears if black boy is a good place, and worth fighting for. For a very long Time a pause, a black boy, something on paper resembles the apparition of wet petals on black boy dangling amidst the others, unblinking their eyes. And because he could not stop for the other black boys, he thought, they kindly stopped for me, knowing all along he will see those best black boys of his generation destroyed by madness, washed out of the turret with a hose held by nobody. He, just a thief—how do black boys crawl into, crawl down alone into the death he has wanted so badly and for so long. Then, driven by the fierce scrutiny of heaven to their election in the vast breath, black boy seeks the rumor of mortality among these pages turning. Black boy, forlorn in the cellar he creates for himself, wanders in some mid-kingdom, when so much depends upon a black boy glazed with rain water beside the white chickens he has never seen alive. He will bring a bouquet of poppies, if he also knows what they look like, knowing black boys are always born in the cruelest month, that the ceaseless weaving of an uneven black boy is a winning cake given to himself on any day but a birthday. And, he cries out, throwing down what could be the final unpublished manuscript by Maurice Blanchot, what I want to know is how do you like your blueeyed black boy Mister Deathly White,

as though awaking from uneasy dreams and finding he had been transformed into a black boy

by standing up, realizing he has somehow forgotten about having legs.

He has been seated on the dirty box for hours. Or what he thinks are hours. Hasn't felt like it. Time's tricky like that in this particular building made and abandoned by white people. He walks around for his poor circulation smarting, and for some other urge he can't identify yet, though it bothers him just as much.

The sunrise spilling through one of the myriad holes in the brick wall opposite him helps sort out his confusion. He's hungry for breakfast soup. Can black boy eat what his dead mother gives him. He has not earned it. Not while ten thousand dead mothers wait for their cursing sons on ten thousand sofas somewhere with leave-come all over them, enveloped in a cloud of clove smoke which will still be there when he slowly turns the knob to the front door, finding it unlocked somehow, the only one out of ten thousand he could possibly come home to without so much as anyone—least of all her—calling out from the living room which does not live but consults the thin televisional voices drowning out the belabored, what he already knows has happened to her because it would, today of all days, after having read a hypothetical unpublished manuscript by a Maurice Blanchot he will never know, his new ur-friend in the aberrant, self-loathing city with lives happy, productive.

He would have been very happy and productive himself, just this once, to share this manuscript with his dead mother who this Time does not stir on the sofa as he enters the room, a grey curl of clove cigarette ash around her middle and index finger, long cold to the room, her scanning eyes fixed to where perhaps she expected her son to be when he returned so it would not take long for him to understand, now, him awaiting the eternal curse which does not arrive like a driverless taxi cab in the afterlife reunion but remains where she lies, not even a thin sheet covering her, any of her, all that he had seen and not seen before, the bruising, the blood, a cloud clearing him, standing in the center of the living room which does not live, bringing the manuscript and its thin pages now thinning further to his chest, nearly crushing, tearing them, and holding them against the beating of his hideous heart which mutters, I myself am Hell, and everyone and he stopped breathing.

THERE ARE SO MANY GENTLE PEOPLE
TO ENTERTAIN IN LOS ANGELES

WHEN YOU ASK ME when am I leaving for Los Angeles, I say I don't know because this is the I that I am talking about. I can only come to Los Angeles with an invitation that is not really an invitation for me but the I. I can only come to Los Angeles with an econo-class plane ticket and a two-star bungalow hotel room in the I's name. I can only come to Los Angeles if Gary Oldman is waiting for the I to stop screwing around and get on with it already. I can only come to Los Angeles if other certain stipulations for the I are met. The I, after all, is demanding of me.

I can only come to Los Angeles if they ask me to leave the aberrant, self-loathing city for another, not an invitation, not a signature, not you, but asking me who sometimes writes to come to Los Angeles and share in the experience of writing in Los Angeles where no writing is ever done despite the multitude of lonely perverts forever wandering hallways for their own anecdotal pleasures, confirmed or no, televisional or radiological, though mostly televisional now. Calls upon calls sent down these hallways I can only imagine for myself, places where ice never grows at the feet but they put fiery coals in my head instead if they like me—especially if they like the I's work—and the only thing painful about it will be the smiling I have to do afterwards. But all of that comes much later. First: plenitude of alcohol without threat of violence. Plenty of plenitude. How you doing. How shitty was the econo-trip. What's going on over at your other building. Have you read this person. What are you up to—meaning, what are you writing. Because no one who writes ever asks another person what they are writing. That's evident. Which is nothing. Evident. Writing, none. There is no writing taking place anywhere. Not in Los Angeles. Just plenitude is all. Some drinks. Catching up. Catching eyes of whomever walking by, maybe someone about to be famous, someone looking for an ur-friend, someone looking for the next Gary Oldman. Of course I know but do not mention that there will never be another Gary Oldman. There will be another Sid Vicious before that ever happens.

Though will I return home the same as how I left. The I has my round-trip econo-class plane ticket. Anecdotes and aberrations belonging to me safely stowed away in the overhead bin. Seat upright. Latest personal technology powered down. There is nothing happening. There is nothing to say as the first round of drinks are poured, the gentle women shuffle through the aisles, and everyone begins to take out their anecdotes while no one is looking, almost all of them involving gentle people who were never gentle people invariably, indiscriminately, but not inconspicuously. It is important to be seen. Anecdotes are about being seen, not necessarily about being heard. In Los Angeles, I have been told, a walking anecdote can go three miles in two steps if it is a particularly skilled one, traveling places, meeting gentle people, entering buildings the like of which I have never seen before, being only accustomed to the Oriental magnificence that is Mann's Chinese Theater while in the presence of your famous sister, though that anecdote I have already worn down with frequent walking and re-walking. I know I will fail resisting that anecdote happening again, like rebooted minstrel shows or the possibility of *The Return of Mork and Mindy*, but remain a Chinese Theater that was never a Chinese Theater like Mann's. That building can always be revisited with new company, new ur-friends, a bevy of lousy habits yet to be celebrated, consecrated by you and you all.

The Los Angeles that exists for Gary Oldman the day he was made into an anecdote for your famous sister has been divided into seven hallways of different colors separate from each other so the chances of lonely perverts being able to cross paths with each other is reduced to a bare minimum. They always manage to find each other, however, the makers of the hallways being unaware of the tunnels which run between them, connected by the work of Gary Oldman which they converse in, line by line of dialogue they imagine themselves speaking in black leather jackets worn by third generation Irish-American criminals or expensive Italian suits or regal Transylvanian attire, smoothing down the Puritan finery as it lays upon their imaginary pale white bodies of resplendent ectomorphism and sunken chest, never now ever finding a Los Angeles off-limits to them, a hallway for every dream, a dream for every Gary Oldman they wanted to be upon watching *Sid and Nancy* when they were a teenager and understood the true nature of a gentle man who is no longer a gentle man, how it takes so much Time, so much care, that the easiest, most charitable thing to do is disappear him forever into one large movie franchise about super-intelligent talking apes no one will remember after they watch it, even if it remains no charity for anyone, including Gary Oldman.

Should I work on the script for the commercial in the I's two-star bungalow hotel room, I will look over my notes for any anecdote to latch onto so I may find the right role for Gary Oldman to slip into instead, so that he may be Gary Oldman again and yet a not-Gary Oldman. This is something which the I hasn't been trained for. Other people have reminded me of this in the form of memos, emails and other communiqués prior to the committees filled with gentle people who express concern over my gentleness, that I may never be able to write Gary Oldman into being for a script which does not exist except for a series of thin typewritten pages and index cards with various insertable banalities such as: emo [Gary Oldman] ruins true love on purpose so that he may find it himself again but this Time on his own terms; or strung out [Gary Oldman] in Rio de Janeiro saved by surprisingly humanistic tribe of Amazonian pygmies stumbles upon vast renewable energy source in the rainforest which he decides not to tell anyone about; or feckless [Gary Oldman] befriends smart-ass anthropomorphic CGI marmot and helps it realize concept of waking reality so that it stands a fighting chance to join civilization and write a novel about the experience. All voices, here, there, not mine, to be sure, but trivial fancies. A room full of bored, tired gentle people who just want to enjoy plenitude, share their anecdotes, and go home to what they think is home, to either ruined love, eternal power or figmentary housepets.

A curtain of steam draws her fingers over me.

In our bathroom mirror my face beads up into questionable emotive droplets you yourself would never confuse with tears as the water laps around me, as I realize I do not normally take hot baths in your presence for obvious reasons, being that it is difficult to scald me while standing up straight in a shower, much less drown me. I see the luxury of this moment, what I have been missing, which was always there, your famous sister, who only wanted to watch *Sid and Nancy* over and over and let it lead to wherever it was going to lead and let me take a bath in peace afterwards where the incipient threat of scalding and drowning has been replaced by a hallway I walk down with whomever I want, though I am still alone, the hand drawing away from mine, proceeding to door to door to hand upon door and a story, there, each one waiting to become that thin reverberation without voice to ruin it all for those of us who wait outside, I, who waits for you, returning, you standing far at the end of the hallway.

I can only come to Los Angeles if Gary Oldman wants the I in that Platonic non-sexual way which always turns sexual regardless. Respects the I's budding work. Reticence for the latest personal technology notwithstanding, there is recognition of mutual benefit if not perfect symbiosis among the wide boulevards and healthy palm trees and unfortunate spandex no one stops wearing ever because Los Angeles never left the 1980's no matter how hard Frank Gehry tried to convince the gentle people otherwise with his non-existent building. Because there are so many of them in the aberrant, self-loathing city, the necessity of entertainment eternal and the signs of such, there can only be so many more who will not be entertained, no matter how hard Gary Oldman tries, no matter how many visits Gary Oldman makes to the Gehry Museum and indirectly entertains those who thought they were only going to the Gehry Museum instead of Mann's Chinese Theater, watching your famous sister try to walk through a plate-glass door as if Gary Oldman was not there.

But Gary Oldman is there. Right now. Waiting. Cursing. Pacing back and forth in a meticulous re-enactment of all the tortured souls he has played before with such élan and stringy hair that he can't help thinking he needs help, should any arrive in the form other than his hairless agent. Not bloody likely, he lapses into his British idiom, nearly spilling his early afternoon bourbon I place from afar in his hand since he usually waits until the evening to drink unless he is writing, when he knows he is alone, considering all the gentle people who, at the moment, wonder what he is doing with himself right then and there. He would very much like to shout at these so-called people. Lunatics with their own moon. The aberrant, self-loathing city breeds them. No one looks up. No one looks for entertainment. The old distractions. Love is all around us. Love, he snorts. Bollocks.

True, it has been awhile since he played any role involving the kind of love shared in *Sid and Nancy*, *Immortal Beloved*, or even *Dracula* in a tangentially related way involving a passionate Victorian-era defense of esoteric necrophilia, relying instead on the love for family, the love for money, even the love for mother Russia or the cold, dutiful love for majestic Britain aligned against Russia colder still, thus cancelling each other out, leaving the tired, empty husk of Gary Oldman to ponder his next move while inwardly grieving the betrayal of his wife with a younger version of himself. What of the big stage. All your mates are doing Broadway, old boy, good work if you can get it— somewhat noble, too, provided you shake the mob outside. The project comes to him: hyper-contemporary revision of *Heart of Darkness* anchored by that Ebola nonsense. Last colorful lunatic role in Kurtz which has eluded his storied career. He'll show those fluffers Brando and Malkovitch how it's done, yeah. Perfect. Where's stationery. There's none. Stay at a fucking five-star hotel in fucking Los Angeles surrounded by fuck-alls meant to cater to every whim and not a single bleeding scrap of paper to jot down fucking genius plans. C'est magnifique. Highball glass of very old super-premium bourbon sails short but direct trajectory into nearest boudoir mirror it can find as if Gary Oldman's hand acts by radar. Further provocation by predictable, gentle knock on the door. Everything all right in there, sir. No. Fuck off. Yes sir I'll do that. You'll do that because you all are shiftless wankers who can't even stock a presidential suite with stationery. Yes sir, that we are—would you like any stationery. No, I'd like to die the most painful death imaginable—didn't I say fuck off already you blooming cunt. Yes sir that you did—I'll let housekeeping know about the stationery mistake, our apologies, Mister Oldman, very sorry about that.

I can only come to Los Angeles with a personal phone call, with an actual phone of the earliest personal technology as the I has stipulated to Los Angeles, a mobile phone with a voice sending me on an econo-class plane across the land of the country filled with the most gentle of people in recorded history and even off the record, places that not even Gary Oldman himself would dare tread lest he had to see for himself the fruition of an American etiquette he helped shaped. No, he should really be getting back to Los Angeles now—got the ape shoot, then the commercial thing, yeah. Right, off we go—and with a harrumph his advancing age betrays to no one who is around he finds himself making calls of minor importance to send out other calls to people he has not been talking to, such as the writers, and get them in soon so we can finish the bloody thing and get on to the über-apes already, which he has a queasy feeling about, keeping a deep-bottomed plastic receptacle handy nearby.

I can only come to Los Angeles if the Gehry Museum does actually exists, if your famous sister was actually there, if you famous sister actually tried walking through a plate-glass door while Gary Oldman watched perturbed and thought, I should do something to help this poor girl, until, as she recognized him, she pulled out her AUTOGRAPHS book, leaving him to reconsider, I should do something to help myself, at the behest of his hairless agent nearby who would rather not have him give his signature but always difficult to stop Gary when he sets his mind to something charitable, he conceded, so let the poor girl have her fun before they straitjacket her, likely forget the whole thing, as we all will, no, really, forget it, it's not a bother, love, just seem to be in some dire straits is all— let me keep you company till help arrives, here you are. Don't forget your pen.

The world-renowned spot where your famous sister bled.

Clean, undescript, any concrete patch of anonymity has been touched by the presence of a Gary Oldman. A Gary Oldman looking down upon the one whom he should have never crossed paths with, never should have witnessed himself and then sign his name to the moment in verification, affixed with her blood which could not be stopped with mere violent alcoholic acting style, but the pity of spectacle unrests something else in her, he knows, he can tell, the sudden hush and pall over recognition of what she has done and what she is about to do, and the moment of clarity, as they say, arrives to both parties involved, so swiftly, suddenly, but not choreographed so that they think it is love but quickly snuff that emotion when they notice the blood running down her arm, making the fabric of her shirt heavy, damp, a pendulum to earth

I am unfamiliar with the motions of the earth and how they may be expressed with heavy, swinging objects, exacting the plumb-line to hang in perfect, unscripted fleeting. Is there any use in saying the motions have their patterns to be mapped and graphed with near-precision should we apply them to a gentle man who is no longer a gentle man hanging at the end of a noose, or the twisted fabric of a wounded desperately searching in a purse for an AUTOGRAPHS book, when the mirror bends on its own motion in full view of the sun, bending, turning its way into a building that wants desperately to not be a building, so much so that it nearly fools Gary Oldman until witnessing the example of his own acting history unfold in the guise of a disturbed young woman who bears some passing resemblance to Chloe Webb, ah, yes, her, been awhile, that, can't say I've thought of her lately but that poor poor woman whatever she was trying to do, with her own motion, bringing her into the world for one last attempt so she could enter a building in the most painful way possible so that she may be able to leave it, leave all of it, and herself in it, just for the benefit of a man she believes is the Gary Oldman of her mundane upstate adolescent existence

and what is belief if not Gary Oldman never entering the Gehry Museum but only in his mind and what is the mind of Gary Oldman but a Gehry Museum that does not exist except for

your famous sister your famous sister your famous sister your famous sister

thinking your famous sister is behind one of the doors, in a room with several subrooms or antechambers watching a worn-down VHS copy of *Sid and Nancy* over and over with a young gentle man of her choice, plucked from the grim vicissitudes of a building neither of them wanted to be in, a hospital in Los Angeles she never wanted to return to even if the young gentle man thought she would be better off there, as I once did, where memory would not be a burden as so much as an ur-friend she would hope to meet in the flesh, outside, where there are no hallways for me to roam, where no one can be anonymous when you ask them for their signature in your AUTOGRAPHS book that signs itself when you put it down on the dresser and, leaving it closed, draw your hand across the faux-pleather cover with AUTOGRAPHS embossed in faux-gold lettering remembering how each occasion the thin faux-paper pages nearly ripped at the harsh impression of a ball-point pen wielded by the hand of none other than Gary Oldman himself, one of her, like, most favorite actors, he had to sign the book don't care whether or not he thinks she was a freak or loony, oh no, but not having the signature would be a death not worth living for if she was to be forever trapped in a room without windows

people forever wandering outside the hallway making comments about her, observing her, remarking to the person next to them

this the woman who collected signatures and put her arm through a plate-glass door at the Gehry because she thought it really wasn't there her sister and boyfriend are coming out from New York to pick her up after discharge may pursue therapy there likely won't happen no I doubt it cant hold her anyway indefinitely should be out already but sitting on her until they get here she won't budge we've made recommendations for facilities elsewhere but they're not involving parents can't notify no not yet maybe when they get here

They won't huh

all the while these considerations pour over notes evaluations observations reports memos logs sign-ins checklists requests signed dated belated unsealed checked signed struckthrough revised attached copied sent sifted sitting waiting waiting, while she keeps the AUTOGRAPHS book which you will receive, which sits in our room, with one anonymous bloody thumbprint by the signature of a Gary Oldman passing by, minding his own business the best he could.

At any given Time there can only be one possible Los Angeles existing at Gary Oldman's behest, the city which only includes your famous sister prostrated at his feet, bleeding, rambling incoherently if not in complete shock, her suggesting the general unknowability of aberrant, self-loathing cities since nothing could be further from its own truth beauty, created for itself in the form of a bending mirror forming a continuous loops of cold meaningless stares from the soles of her shoes that no one, not even she, can read. That a puddle of blood forms is the only proof that she ever stood there, Gary Oldman sees, thinking of all the puddles of blood he had to stand in once wardrobe was finished and they got the mascara right, finally. That was a fine thrill, he reflects, letting out his finest bellows and curses while losing sight of whose blood he was really standing in (it could never be his own, after all), a blood to take him where he really needed to be at that particular moment, Paris, Bangkok, Moscow, London, New York especially. Especially not so special as he preferred but its generosity assumed the form of those he had known, such as Chloe Webb, who wasn't so bad, except she was Nancy Spungen, and that was bad enough in the bathroom at the Chelsea, how many takes it took her to realize she should look into the mirror first before collapsing in a pool of her own blood which wasn't her own blood but a sort of transubstantiated Nancy Spungen only the Hotel Chelsea could afford while he slept on the bed as Sid Vicious would, dreaming mightily of phone jacks and coffee cups and himself being swallowed in general by large cavernous objects representing the sort of cockroach he thought he would wake up as and have other gentle people be terribly ashamed about until Nancy Spungen awoke, rising from the pool of her own blood at the end of her journey, springing to her feet first and stretching her young body, looking at him lovingly, smiling, grateful that she doesn't have to look into the mirror ever again.

The I has an ur-friend in Los Angeles who is not so easily entertained.

There are screams and predilections and so impressive saying nothing does this ur-friend stand without the countenance betraying entertainment or edification or both. An act of betrayal. A signature on a contract. A statement of intent, personal in nature or impersonal or both. A commitment. A curse. All airport terminals look the same. All preclude themselves before the passengers. The only thing remaining of me is my ur-friend in Los Angeles. Chest slowly rising, falling. I place my hand there. Thirty thousand feet. Only a part. Can I get another. I'll have to check first. Someone is waiting. Someone is willing. I have a sofa if you need it, you know, to crash. I'll have to check first. These things must be cleared because Gary Oldman is waiting, though reluctant bride the I is. And no one gets married in Los Angeles. Entertainment, edification, or both. A commitment. A curse. An act of betrayal. A building. Institution is said. Gary Oldman is meant.

There are so many gentle people to entertain in Los Angeles is the day when the I sits and tries to write a commercial in this two-star bungalow hotel room so I may impress many people with a televisional voice for Gary Oldman's inevitable presence in a primetime television drama later as America's newest ur-friend, though there are so many people to impress—that is, for each episode—and I wonder if the I could write them all into a script where Gary Oldman and I— that is, for each episode—talk to people, not realizing that there are too many who do not have to be impressed to be entertained, unlike you and you all, too many who will never want to be on primetime so that all the famous people who are not Gary Oldman can watch them and pity them and hate them—that is, episode by episode—a self-congratulatory hate for avoiding the writing the I is doing now, at night, in Los Angeles, away from you away from me writing every manuscript which will not be published to the hypothetical joy of those waiting to be entertained with the closest, nearest, but not basest approximation of a Gary Oldman they all love like their own child.

The episode of hate the I writes for a Gary Oldman who is not yet entertained takes place at a Gehry Museum which is not yet a Gehry Museum but only the idea of it suggested by people waiting to be impressed by something by waiting for it without being conscious of it, recognizing only the violent alcoholic acting style of a Gary Oldman circa *The Professional* since *Sid and Nancy*, on the other hand, along with *State of Grace*, *The Fifth Element* and *Air Force One* are deemed efforts of low cultural import which has neither impressed nor entertained many people, much to the disappointment of a Gary Oldman who needs little pretense to create a Gehry Museum with little or no culture whatsoever, but decides to linger further, lighting a cigarette he will tell his hairless agent that he did not light, at the risk of someone coming along and being impressed with his ability to light a cigarette on the sidewalk and be so utterly unentertained unless a person he truly hates comes along and asks for his autograph while completely ignoring the fact that a beautiful building of cultural import stands before them.

Gary Oldman Is a Building I Must Walk Through, the I will write for the pilot episode title up until the last tearful farewell watched by all of America as a significant event of cultural importance.

Gary Oldman is a building I must walk through because this is what Gary Oldman wants more than anything, for myself, for you and you all, for the gentle people who do not have to be impressed to be entertained desire a building of their own to walk through, to place their hands on the doors and feel the thin reverberations of televisional and radiological voices they think will be their ur-friends. Instead, I will make those voices not televisional or radiological but of the flesh which holds not open doors, which is gentle not to the touch of wrought iron and the fairness of balconies in the rain, which will sign its own name knowing that name's significance is only a story for people who can never be entertained and thus wish to continue to do so, a curtain which never drops, the very touching music which never plays, the triumphant end credits which never roll, the season premiere of a life which never compares to the actual Gary Oldman as he walks down the hallway

and Gary Oldman walking down the hallway is a Gary Oldman who the gentle people who are entertained have never seen before, who they would pay good money to watch—maybe even excellent money—though all for naught since the building Gary Oldman walks through holds only himself, and no one else. At last, he thinks, tired, hunted, hounded by the specters of ten thousand famous sisters who are not yours who share with each other the names they have collected, greedily, inspiring only to those who understand the macabre intent of owning names so they may be conjured at will like a succubus for all their dreams and desires to inhabit and animate it, a name which will plead fidelity, honesty, and, most of all, entertainment to the one who has called it forth, the one who walked many hallways for this moment, the one who has bled from the incredulity of waiting that resists the plate-glass door granting access to the only building the name-bearer needs to enter ever again, breathless

the name of your famous sister never to be mentioned again, I had wanted to say to you on so many occasions you and I sat next to each other on the sofa with the windows open, listening to the sirens outside and doing our best not to think of the gentle man who is no longer a gentle man, but I did not have to say it because I think we both knew we were in the building there with him, waiting for the end of him like he waited for the end of her to arrive so he could join her in the afterlife reunion and on and on, never realizing her name would not be mentioned again because of this waiting, because we knew the windows would always be open, the sirens always sounding from some neighborhood adjacent to ours, and if we could have left the building, we would have done it right then and there, we would have moved on once the story was told and continue, and instead we waited for the next episode. We waited for continuance, complication, copulation, resolution. We waited for the episode to come kill us in our sleep, caught *in flagrante delicto* in bed with another, younger episode.

The I has an ur-friend waiting for me at the Gehry Museum that will someday exist

if it exists outside of Gary Oldman, a someone who is there to be there, for me, a someone who should not be in Los Angeles without you, I think, and yet here I am—come and take me, Gary Oldman, take me by the hand, here I am, won't you show me who I am along ten thousand raised eyebrows in a single continuous video loop which never stops playing at the Gehry Museum where no one pays any attention. The lights are out, the workers have gone home, the doors are closed. There is only one way to enter. The darkened Gehry Museum I stand outside of is only darker for the ur-friend who I know is in there, waiting for me to oblige my contractual obligations to the building I have never been to and only know from the lore of your famous sister narrating, which is also the lore of *Sid and Nancy*, which must forever be the lore of a Gary Oldman who once did not care for commercial shoots or even Los Angeles itself but your famous sister instead, however fleeting it was. And the fleeting it was, stays. A farewell look as the ambulance doors closed. The suggestion of fireworks as the lights bounced off the mirrored exterior for everyone to watch since Gary Oldman was long gone, whisked away by his hairless agent, the rapidity of accommodation, a bourbon waiting somewhere for unwinding purposes. Fleeting, you know, says Gary Oldman. Just a thought. Poor girl. Someone inside is sure she'll be all right. Someone inside, waiting, to say it will be all right. Everything. That the building once was everything cannot be fleeting, or even a fleeting thing, not for chasing it down knowing it could never be caught, not for celebrating something which had no event but only an anecdote, a way of telling. It is dark outside is only another way of telling an ur-friend is waiting to tell me it will be outside, and that is when the darkness will cease being darkest.

That is when everyone will see my face.

What amuses me over the potential existence of the Gehry Museum in Los Angeles is its construction of ten thousand plate-glass doors I recognize immediately as I approach it as your famous sister must have approached it before thinking she met Gary Oldman, a building whose facade is meant to deceive people who walk into plate-glass doors, like Gary Oldman as Sid Vicious, into thinking they can enter anywhere, like Sid Vicious as Gary Oldman, and become part of a significant cultural work, unlike Mann's Chinese Theater, which, to be sure, has its own plate-glass doors which one can enter with, but the sheer number of actual and implied plate-glass doors constitutes a form of architectural one-upmanship that vintage Hollywood destinations cannot stand up to, albeit these destinations are secretly relieved that then thousand Sid Viciouses won't be paying a visit anytime soon, only myself, that is, who for the longest tie never wanted to resemble Sid Vicious in any way, never desired walking through a plate-glass door, never considered himself anything but a narrator to you and your famous

sister, I who am bereft of the experience of a violent alcoholic background and significant cultural appreciation, visiting a building which only exists in the mind of someone whom I have never met if only I may know, rather obliquely, not the futility of existence but existing in a failed etiquette I have narrated others in and narrate myself in as I approach the building

I must walk through thinking, for you

I would never do this because not once have I dedicated myself to anything for anyone, not all attuned to this dedicational and epigraphical living which somehow sums up our lives in pithy aphorisms or sentient quotes from culturally significant people who have walked through the building with their lives intact, their sanity in its rightful place, their face in one piece, and without so much as a hint of blood, and if I fail doing this now

walking through the plate-glass door at the Gehry Museum which only
exists in the mind of Gary Oldman, I know, unlike your famous sister, Gary
Oldman will not be there to comfort me as he stands over me, wondering what
I was

thinking and would I care for his autograph before his hairless agent whisks
him away unto the undeserved obscurity of an etched highball glass filled
with bourbon and leather chair and fireplace somewhere in the Los Angeles
countryside before I quickly, decisively, but not cleanly grab his hand before
he has the opportunity to find the writing implement of his choice and recite
every word, every lone of dialogue from every Gary Oldman film I can
remember and remind him

every commercial was once a poem and once a poem becomes Gary Oldman
it belongs to him and him alone to recite in the afterlife reunion while he waits
for your famous sister to arrive in a driverless taxi cab while being serenaded
by a throng of black boys with a boom box and the eternal curse on their lips
silenced by the gesture of the glass I break walking through the door with
everyone, no one watching while it happens, finding there not the ice I had
expected dropping to one knee but all the cultural significance a building can
muster being made of ten thousand mirrors that will never break under the
mindless attention of ten thousand Sid Viciouses but have broken under me

now narrator of luxuriated myself no longer caring what happens to the
audience of you all standing and listening to the sound of broken glass at my
feet sounding the pit-pit from blood falling upon the shards as I stand warily,
bemusedly, but not certainly for thinking I had done what your famous sister
could not, checking my arm, looking at the palms of my hands which once
held you on our sofa, signing myself over and over into you

now narrator of myself no longer walking but carrying me into the marbleized
lobby where an audience of security awaits to care for me, tend to my every

need, but never my desire to make the Gehry Museum exist for a Gary Oldman I have never met and have never narrated with a full sense of who Gary Oldman is, not until I walk through this building that your famous sister never could

now narrator of bloody myself no longer blinking at the harsh florescent lights of the building, at the cold marbleized interior of the building, at the implied cultural significance of the building, at the roofless architecture a drunken Sid Vicious could never have thrown himself from, at the audience of security only being an audience to me signing the floor with myself in a steady pit-pit down the hallway, down, alone, a din of voices voicing a stare belonging only to an ur-friend until the very end

a sofa in-of-itself of implied cultural significance if not utility, though it does seat for me, slippery pleatherly yet

the artwork Gary Oldman never was audience to because of your famous sister—or because of his hairless agent because of your famous sister—never realizing he never had to be the audience when all that he does narrates my sitting here, bleeding, looking at a painting

requiring no narration I could provide for myself or for you or for you all or even Gary Oldman were he to chance upon me sitting in this wing slowly bleeding with him powerless to do anything about it despite all those violent alcoholic roles where the power he had undid him by the end in some way his helplessness now the best ur-friend I have ever had to myself to narrate here before all the gentle people come crushing down the hallway just to get a glimpse of the famous Gary Oldman putting his comforting hand on the shoulder of someone bleeding to death on a sofa after walking through a plate-glass door like Sid Vicious in *Sid and Nancy* so he could leave the Gehry Museum with Gary Oldman by his side an afterlife reunion which does not have to take place in the afterlife does not require a final unpublished manuscript to tell you about the eternal curse of black boy serenading me as I am led away carried away in an ambulance to enter the last building I will never leave because you will not be waiting for me

not like Gary Oldman, sighing,

It's going to be all right, son.

I LACK THE FORGIVENESS
OF GARY OLDMAN

ONCE I WANTED

I could not begin so I wanted. I never once said, You say. Tell me. I have
no stories. Never once. I went home once. I found you there. Sleeping. On
our sofa. Windows open. Lights off. Reading me. A letter. A manuscript.
A bloody thumb-print. This is what happened. You said you were
sleeping. I do not know. Once I read you. I was not sleeping. I went out
for a walk. A reading, some would say. A sleeping, others. Every face a
story. Every story a bloody you. I stopped to look. Or stooped, some
would say. I was not talking. I was not listening. Your narrator, I did not
say. Tell me not. Did you sleep for me. Gary Oldman does not sleep. His
hairless agent won't let him. You won't let me. I stopped to say. I stooped
to listen. I won't let you. I won't tell you. I was talking. I was listening.
Ten thousand faces in the aberrant, self-loathing city. It was not enough.
It was not sleeping. All said. You said. Your narrator. Our sofa. Windows
open. Lights off. A reading, some would say. A sleeping, others. I could
not sleep. Once I said I slept to you and you replied, Never. You went out.
Took a walk. A constitution, some have said. A jaunt, others. I was with
you once, I say. Not looking. No famous sister. An aberrant, self-loathing
city. The lowest level before our feet touch the ice. A story where none are
told. Only anecdotes. Suffering. You took my joy, you said. Only once. It

was enough. It was not forever. Once you wanted me. Only you never said this. Gary Oldman, you said. You were him once. Not I. He was enough. He was forever. What was the trick, I say. You know. Personality. Charm. Good looks. Talent. Leniency. Joy, but only once. Once as Sid Vicious. An aberrant, self-loathing happiness. An eternal curse. Everyone said. You were not looking. You were with me once, you say. You could not begin so I told you a story. About Gary Oldman as Sid Vicious. As your famous sister. As everyone. Take a walk. I can't sleep. I can't say. I took your once. I have your never. I say. It was enough. It was forever. What is forever. I do not know. Suffering, has been said. Joy, others. Perhaps I, your narrator. I do not say. I do not say I to others—least of all you. What am I to you. An anecdote. An autograph. An aberration. Some trick of a word. Some geedee. I know a few. Least of all you. Another trick. Another day. I went out looking for a story. Gary Oldman, has been said. Your famous sister, others. And others more still. What has been all said. I do not know. I do not say. I, your narrator. All said, I have said something. About Gary Oldman. About your famous sister. About you. About gentle men no longer gentle. About our upstairs neighbor. About Maurice Blanchot. About the black boy. Perhaps. Did I say something about geedee. I do not know. I do not say geedee to others. Least of all to geedee. What am I to you. A building. A hallway. A door. I went through one looking for a story. All I found was Gary Oldman. All said, I say the I. About I, a story. But I am not Gary Oldman, you say. Are you a narrator. Suffering, has been said. Joy, others. You do not know. You do not say. Another trick. Another day. You went out looking for your famous sister. You found a building. I was there. Not Gary Oldman. Your narrator, all said. The I says I, not you. You put your hand on my chest. You say, Not you. And others more. I do not know, I say. I was here. Still. But I am not your famous sister. I am not a story. What am I to you, I say. A narrator. An ur-friend. You do not say. All said, you have a few anecdotes. And Gary Oldman. Forgive me, you say. You found a hallway. You found a door. I was not there. You say me, not I. You went out looking for me. You found geedee. Another trick. Another day. I do not know. I do not say. All said. Still. I know a story. Not forgiveness. Least of all you. You said. And I said you. Not Gary Oldman. Not your famous sister. That is not a day, I know. You say you do not. And others more.

Suffering. Joy. I was not here. I was in Los Angeles. I found a building, I say. Not your famous sister. I do not say Gary Oldman. Not now. Not ever. But I should say Gary Oldman, the I. Know your narrator. Not me, you know. Do not say I to me. Least of all you. You are not here. A building says here, all said. Not I. Your narrator should say something gentle—a building, for instance. You in it. Not Gary Oldman. Not a story. Not me, no. I am here, I say. In a building. In a room. In a bed. Not on a sofa. Ours. Voices. Suffering. Joy. Perhaps I do not say. You should say something here. Your hand on my chest. Beauty. Truth. Not me. No. What am I to you, you say, I. Another trick. Another day. A voice in the hallway said. An opening door does not. Only I. Only your gentle hand. You are not here, I say. But I should say Gary Oldman. In a building. In a room. In your bed. Do not say your to me. Least of all you. I am not there. I went out looking for you. I did not find geedee. What is all said to I, your narrator, you know. I know people, some have said. You, others. I do not know. Gary Oldman, I say. He is here. He is forever. A sleeping. A reading. A stooping. The design of a building. He went inside. He found himself, he didn't say. He did not know. I, for instance. The plate-glass door. The stairs up up up. The rooftop—the view to an aberrant, self-loathing city. And below the hallways and doors of every dream to be. He knows them. He knows them all. He forgives them all. He would forgive Sid Vicious if Sid Vicious would let him. Violent alcoholic personalities seldom acquiesce. See, here's a rooftop, Sid, he would say. You own it. You forgive yourself. Nancy, too. Stooping. Would I. I do not know. I only know people. Is it enough. Every door we enter could forgive. Gentle people only hold it open. That can't be I, all said. That can't be forever. Fucking hell. Below he knows them all. See, here's a wanker. Oi. Up up up. He does not hear him. He had gone for a walk. Now this. It is never enough. They all know. Least of all him. A sleeping. A reading. A slouching. He owns it. It does not forgive him. Perhaps I should leave. He wants to look for a story. There are enough already, all say. Gary Oldman knows. He leaves himself. He sleeps. He dreams of a phone jack. Other earliest personal technology. What is a building without. A building without a door, some would say. Nothing, others. He can't hear them. I won't let him. I won't. I walk. I leave. All these faces. Too many dreams. Beauty. Truth. Do not say. It will be enough. It won't be forgiveness, I know. That much. You can't hear me. You are not here. You are your famous sister. Before or after. I do not know. I do not know your famous sister. I do not know Nancy Spungen. Only the building. Only the resemblance. Too many floors. Too many rooms. A voice for every reading. When is check-out. What is forever. I remember your hand on my chest. I do not know if I deserved it. You agreed once. You went for a walk. You hated the neighborhood. Your famous sister hated me. Despite me. I knew Gary Oldman. It was not enough. For her I had your hand. A sofa for every touching. The windows kept open. Never a breeze. Not here. It came on the sirens. It took its Time. I remember knowing. Your voice was her only resemblance. Aren't you ashamed. I agreed once. You hated me for it. Before there was a building here. It was not Gary Oldman afterwards. Not enough floors. Not enough rooms. A voice for every sofa. Resembling a siren. Deserving a breeze. Taking its Time. Forever. You and I went for a walk once. Gary Oldman said it was enough. The lowest level. The people who work in this building. Another trick. Another day. Blinds are drawn. Beds are made. You say. I do not know. There is only the sofa. It is enough to talk. To be this gentle. With you. Perhaps. You went out looking for your famous sister. You came back with me. No one knew anything. No one was a day. The people you work with. The black boy. The reading. The voice. The curse. Gary Oldman says it is not enough. Goes against his training. He knows your famous sister. Everyone does. With you. With a walk. In a city. In a building. Ten thousand gentle people for every sofa. No one knows anyone, all said. But you know Gary Oldman, you say. Isn't that enough. With your famous sister. Perhaps. If I talk long enough. If I put them in a driverless taxi cab at the end. Blinds are drawn. Beds are made. I came back with a pizza. I said it was enough. You did not talk. There was only the sofa. There was only you and I. You say. You read. You leave. What of it. I am here. Stooping, your hand does not reach my chest. Gary Oldman, I say. He knows us. You know. He is forever. Not I. It is best if you say, Enough. Not for me. Your famous sister went for a walk. Gary Oldman held the door open. I am gentle, he says. I forgive. It is best if I say, Forever. You do not know. It has not been a problem. It has not been a day. Did you know my story. A walk too long. A bath too hot. A sofa too gentle. And all the buildings I can enter. It is best if he says, Bollocks. He does not know. What is a story. It is best if we say nothing. All said. You came back. A door is forever open, some have said. It is never enough, I say. It is never gentle. Your hand in the water. Enough for saying, Story. It forgives best. It's not a problem. It's best if you come back later. Did you know my problem, he says. It has not been a day. Yet he knows a story. I am gentle, he says. I forgive. It is best if I say nothing. A story is not anyone. Does not hold a door open. Does not walk through a building. Yet you came back, he says. How gentle of you. It is best if you say, Enough. You leave to see me. The building. The door. The stairs. The rooftop. Up up up. It is enough. That much. Some have said. Too much, others. People know the story. Going for a walk. Leaving. I have to let you, all said. I am not there. I am in a building with no doors. So to say. An instance. An anecdote. A gentle man who is no longer gentle. Not him, he knows. He should know you. I should hate you. The way Gary Oldman hates your famous sister. I do not, I say. If not forgiveness. Mann's Chinese Theater. Walking the boulevard. Arm in arm. I should not hate you. The heat, the steam. Gary Oldman has never done a naked bath scene. He has been seen in bikini underwear. I saw you in a bikini once. Only once. Only a beach too cold that day. Of so many which did not. Hand in hand. That's not a day. Some evening when we are alone. Through the steam. Gary Oldman hates me. I know. I forgive him. He should not forgive me. The Gehry Museum. Everywhere Los Angeles forever. Famous underwear. Worn. Only once. Too cold to sleeping together on the sofa. Pressing hands into concrete. Good place to stoop. Good place to drown in a bathtub. This happens often. People forget where they are. Situational awareness. The steam, the mirror. Your stare. You should not hate me. I should drown in the forgiveness of Gary Oldman. Only once. She saw Gary Oldman but he was not there. If not at the Gehry Museum. He has been seen there. I know. A bath too cold. Heatless. Steamless. I know. Some hate only drowns in the skin. The rest forgives. That's not a trick. That's not a day. That's not forever

the I wanted.

EEEEVVVVRRRRYYYYOOOONNNNEEEE;
OR, THE ETERNAL CURSE

SPEAK TO ME—

speak, Gary Oldman's non-voice from the television. Speak a thin, televisional gentle person. Another, more mature Gary Oldman I want to hear over the other voices in this room and am not accustomed to, with cropped haircut, well-manicured facial hair, and world-weary look in his eyes easily mistaken for general apathy. Speak in a commercial of this latest personal technology I am not familiar with that the Gary Oldman tries to sell using an ironic inflection of a new, reformed Gary Oldman wearing a clean, form-fitting t-shirt in a darkening urban penthouse suite, who asks you and you all to not believe what he refers to as *the hype* surrounding this latest personal technology he is not actually selling because he is not actually speaking, his mouth not moving except to me, here, in these hallways the gentle people who work here say I must walk through as the last loneliest pervert in Time.

When you are done not-speaking to me, Gary Oldman's non-voice from the television, when you are done not-speaking the lines I did not write for you for this commercial, the lines I did not spend over three months drafting and re-drafting so they could be not-spoken in less than thirty seconds, the lines completely devoid of a violent alcoholic past, of any memory of Gary Oldman as Sid Vicious, then I myself will know you are indeed my best ur-friend in this building.

The non-voice of Gary Oldman as my best ur-friend is trying to tell me that Gary Oldman never actually speaks, he has never actually spoken, and that every instance of him on film where his lips move to deliver a line is a complete fabrication, as I have learned sitting on this sofa, watching this television in this building. No, instead his dialogue is being delivered by a form of pre-empted telepathy resembling a nonsequential Kung Fu film dubbing: Gary Oldman's voice speaks in conventional voice the lines elsewhere in a hermeneutically sealed recording studio first, then these lines are recorded, then he is whisked away to the shoot location to deliver his lines by only moving his lips, finally adding his recorded voice in post-production, hence achieving the Gary Oldman effect you all know and love when you all become disembodied by listening to his face. The important thing, however, is that this non-voice must always be synchronized with the actual Gary Oldman later so that it is, in fact, Gary Oldman you all are hearing, the violent alcoholic ethos of a man who has entertained us often and very well, our most intimate ur-friend, confiding, secretive, passionate, ready to envelop us in his necromantic green mist of sexual inversion as an apocryphal quasi-Jesus with wire-rim glasses tinted cobalt, warning us of the non-voice which will take us away from what has wounded us the most if not latched to its dear host ten thousand trips down a hallway vaguely familiar to one that has been shared over and over until it may seem strange to the very touch of a hand on a door leading to a Gary Oldman sitting in a real leather chair watching television not saying anything though his lips are moving, and thus not-speaks in the room to supply the voice by his non-voice which speaks only when I narrate it to you, you who are in another hallway, another building, where ten thousand mirrors steam up and no one can wipe them with a hand to reveal this Gary Oldman walking up behind you without saying a single word I can use for your benefit in avoidance, not until he raises an eyebrow. The rest follows silence.

Would the non-voice of Gary Oldman never not-speak to me. Will I know it not for silence but all the other voices I have tried to follow, to make mine, crowding around me in lament that there has never been a Gary Oldman and there never will be—even though I know. I know there has been a Gary Oldman I have watched over and over with your famous sister, speaking to one of us, if not both of us, until he not-speaks without using his lips, merely a glance, a smirk needed to speak not that which doesn't need speaking to the needs of a Gary Oldman who needs nothing but mere silence to show the world that he is indeed Gary Oldman forever, as is the cursing cigarette which dangles unlit from his lips.

Someone who works in this building comes in to turn off the television and personally escort me to my room, a gentle person who is not as gentle as he thinks he is. He is here with me, with his softening, cooing voice radiating what he thinks is positive holistic energy as he reminds me of curfew. This is a curfew inside a building, not outside, I note, to make sure I return to my room before a certain Time unless phone calls are made, reinforcements sent, and a host of gentle people surround me while I am on the sofa and they all look at me with those white dead eyes to move me—here, leaving me with only an entreaty, asking for five more minutes to see if this commercial for the latest personal technology I wrote the script for appears. I think Gary Oldman is even in it, I tell this gentle person, but he may not actually talk in it. Something I pitched to the producer. Proud of the idea, it's different, especially for Gary Oldman, I lie to him, but I will do anything to brush aside this gentle person's assistance so I may present the appearance of my hearing the thin televisional voices say that Gary Oldman is soon arriving to tell me all I have done is arrive in a building you knew was made for me because it was also made for your famous sister when she had something to live for. Any gentle person already knows this. This one does, too, perhaps. He looks at me somewhat kindly, as if thinking he is about to do me a huge favor, as if watching television has ever done a favor for anyone. He nods gently, carefully, but not appreciatively, and he says something that could be vaguely construed as a reasonable response to my lackadaisical attitude towards a curfew which takes place inside a building. The important thing, however, is he does leave me alone with the television on. This is always the important thing. This is what you and you all always do. Otherwise, how would I be able to do the opposite of what I had supposedly been trying to do—in which case, I get up from the sofa and turn the television off before returning to my room. It is the last on the left of an overlong hallway with too few doors to put my hand upon.

*

Though the television remains off, I will sometimes break curfew, leave my room and come back to this sofa, knowing the particular rules and schedules of this building, knowing the people who work in this building are long gone, in the darkness of a building no different than any other darkness I have walked through, to look at the television's blank screen and find Gary Oldman patiently waiting for me.

Gary Oldman is not a gentle man accustomed to waiting in patience, especially for the likes of lonely perverts such as myself. His arms and legs are crossed as any other gentle man would compose his body who is about ready to stop becoming a gentle man because someone had tried to make him speak what he did not want to speak and, in effect, force him to use his non-voice instead, thus depriving the world of the last, greatest incarnation of Gary Oldman wandering the final phase of a failed American etiquette, and creating an impediment to him finding the succor of his life's work and the rewards entitled to him for many colorful roles which entertain us like no other Gary Oldman can, all for thinking perhaps he was indeed Sid Vicious and could avoid the sort of self-aggrandizement which brought down Sid like a lead balloon filled with the heaviest air of Nancy Spungen and a violent alcoholic love that proved too much to overcome, unlike Gary Oldman. He overcame it all: the hardships, the sacrifices, the cleaning up of his image, the crummy parts he had to take later with his career winding down and fewer violent alcoholic roles left to play because you all do not enjoy violent alcoholic roles anymore. He has earned full title and privilege to attempt selling the latest personal technology with an ironic non-voice. I do not hate him at all for it, I tell him. No I don't.

Then why do you have me here, he does not ask me, annoyed. There is no gun to reach for. No bottle to throw. No bead curtain to emerge from. No music in both of our heads.

Remembering the conversation rules of this particular building, I consider what my answer is about to be carefully, cautiously, but not expeditiously.

Gary Oldman, to the best of what you and you all will agree is my corrupted memory, has never been involved in a commercial until this—no business class flights, no Japanese whiskey, no Swedish modern design chairs, nothing. Should I be worried about him. Is he in dire financial straits. Or is his winding down here perfectly natural, in a narratological sense and many other senses, feeling the tension of audience begin to melt into that final recognition of how it is all supposed to wrap up. Then, unexpectedly, Gary Oldman is asked to shoot a commercial for the latest personal technology which I must write his dialogue for, an event of no small significance for me though, since it happens at this particular point in Time, I am a little confused as to how I should receive this development, and I start casting sidelong stares at the televisional Gary Oldman about to read my lines,

You're about to hear some things I'm going to say about this latest personal technology which I've never used before but, before I do so, I want to mention something about your famous sister, which I know you've already heard much about already but bear with me and my voice,

and waiting for these lines I feel an anticipation never felt since I last anticipated your feet touching the ice with mine, only to realize that you and I never did, or you never wanted to, that it was too difficult to return to the hallways to look for her, return to the nodding heads and faces, to the social building where you wait for the black boy to return with a hypothetical unpublished manuscript by Maurice Blanchot and tell you what he read, what he found that would return him to this world without a curse on his lips to inflict upon you anymore, for all of eternity.

Though his non-voice has cancelled every single line of dialogue I had written for him, it is impossible to curse someone who has entertained me so thoroughly, so frequently. This is why, I imagine, it is easy for you to hate me beyond the fact that I am not Gary Oldman, nor will I ever be Gary Oldman, nor will I ever count among my ur-friends the Gary Oldman who met your famous sister during a chance encounter at the Gehry Museum if it existed, which may or may not have happened, not a Gary Oldman who has always helped you select the latest personal technology. You are overwhelmed, let's say, overwhelmed by the masses in general, given your selected occupation with those who are forever occupied with whatever is passing through their minds, unable to find that last gentle impulse which will return them to the etiquette and allow them, among other things, to purchase the latest personal technology being sold by a Gary Oldman who does not move his lips when he speaks. You know that he can speak to them through the thin televisional voice of someone who has rescinded his violent alcoholic past for something more affirming, lucrative, gentle to the mind's eye. The reassuring qualities of stability you all have never seen from Gary Oldman. Today he has given all of us his last, best incarnation where he refrains from the eternal curse that those of us who know Gary Oldman know well which reverberates, etc., etc., that cry of frustration of having to explain oneself perpetually to those who do not know, of having to be forced to rely on others stronger, better equipped than oneself to handle, for instance, an invincible Italian pedophile hitman, knowing that invincible Italian pedophile hitmen are harder to eradicate than, for instance, multiple Sid Viciouses and other self-abused people prone to walking through plate-glass doors.

In the complete, utter absence of that curse, I tell Gary Oldman he is here because he will put down the latest personal technology he is trying to give the world. I will have him walk off set, leave the penthouse suite where he is shooting this commercial, ignoring the Cockney pleas of the director to wrap up this bloody goddamn mess already, and have him head to the rooftop where he will see in all its glory the aberrant, self-loathing city in its anonymity whose name escapes him right now while sitting down because it has been a long evening shooting. There he will see what the eternal curse has given birth to, treading upon the ears of every gentle person who has never heard of Sid Vicious or even *Sid and Nancy*, but knows the Gary Oldman which forms and shapes and defines their lives beyond the latest personal technology and holds illimitable dominion over all—or something terribly dramatic and apocalyptic like that.

As you and you all might have noticed by now, I am not terribly dramatic or apocalyptic in my conveyances, nor do I believe in endings where everyone who was never gentle to begin with is bleeding from every single pore and orifice in their body since narrative must always be selective about pores and orifices as is it selective about people. No, it can't be everyone, Gary Oldman thinks, considering whether his violent alcoholic life really ended when he met that strange, disturbed young woman at what he thought was the Gehry Museum who looked like Chloe Webb who was not bleeding from every pore and orifice but only a select few, who seemed to him the most familiar person he had ever met in his life, finding now the memory alone to be unsatisfactory and the prospect of returning to Los Angeles to relive the moment also unsatisfactory, here, outside this building, while shooting this absurdly pretentious commercial for an overpriced smartphone that will be obsolete by the end of the year and someone else famous will have to do this all over again and find within themselves the Gary Oldman to pass muster to all the desires connected to all the pores and orifices desiring to bleed if they, too, pass through the plate-glass door only to find the latest personal technology is the eternal curse of someone standing alone on the rooftop of a building he will have to leave sometime, in some way, sick to death of his mind feeding upon itself, looking for the way out, when so many others have done it and done it better than anything he can consider right now beyond something someone once wrote in a book he is sure he has never read before.

The notion of suicide would be easier than usual to accomplish in Gary Oldman's thoughts had he (a) drunk a whole bottle of vodka first, (b) coerced another's hand to do what is unfathomable to that gentle person, or (c) fall back on one of his many colorful roles which anticipate something like suicide but never happen as such, only an involuntary death achieved by outside forces instead—a violent explosion, for instance, either by an invincible Italian pedophile hitman detonating a full grenade belt or an ironic Time bomb he himself left onboard an intergalactic luxury cruise ship, both purely unintended consequences. Furthermore, since Gary Oldman is not in possession of a hypothetical unpublished translated novel by Maurice Blanchot, nor is he familiar with Blanchot's law of (un)return, it will be difficult—though not impossible—for him to understand this is one such ending your famous sister had faced, here, on a rooftop just like this, as she not-waited for a gentle man to arrive, that this is an end many gentle people have faced at some point in their lifetime, on the rooftop of a building which looks over everything but reveals nothing to the audience, not by the mere physicality of perspective and elevation but the being outside the building which strips away all anecdotal behavior until a person is left with two very simple options,

Go back inside sober and finish shooting

or

Jump sober and finish shooting

and if by jumping sober not anticipating the physicality of death but his own removal as narrator of the continuous loop set in motion by playing Sid Vicious very well as gentle people who enjoy movies have it, he may thus seal the failed etiquette in a more appropriate fashion than, let's say, natural causes because Gary Oldman can be nothing if he is only natural. On the other hand, he thinks, no man truly believes he will die until the very moment of his death, as a certain philosopher has it. Therefore, anticipating physicality, even in Los Angeles, would appear to be a foregone conclusion on every level of human perception.

I've read too much, Gary Oldman thinks. Reading is the source of all unhappiness. But remember Sid, old boy. Not a reader. Not much of anything. That bloke had it coming, and then you played him. You're the one who went along with the idea of him leaving forever into some bloody stupid afterlife reunion.

He kicks at an imaginary pebble. Looks up because he feels very old at this occurring.

Pretty sky here hey. Stars out.

Caught in between these two choices without a black boy or even Virgil to guide him, I have Gary Oldman stop and wait. He lights a cigarette despite his trying to quit recently. Attempts remembering someone he once crossed paths with, but never knew for himself.

No, it was not me pulling away the veil to make him see the stars. I have no such power. I have no such inclination, yet I must have an ending all the same because that is what you want more than anything. At the end could reside a hate if you decide to not think of me again (and should I ever find out). There is some resentment on my part, too, I admit. Unlike a certain Italian gentle man who believes he is going somewhere in this life worth all the trouble, I am no further along the path than when I started. At the end come the evaluations, the recriminations, adulations, condemnations, or complete and utter indifference. At the end Gary Oldman leaves in a shout, a curse for the world no one hears but me, not profane, not the least bit dirty, a curse for the Gary Oldman trying to sell me something I have already been buying in his name.

This must be the end of Gary Oldman because this is Gary Oldman I am talking about, who, no matter what colorful role he plays, keeps ending himself, like everyone else.

Then again, haven't I always been talking about him ending. I have tried not to talk about myself too much, at least. It's not easy. Why would I change things now just because he is almost finished with this lousy, no-account day. Besides, I think I have done well enough. Or I have done something, at least. Any ending involving Gary Oldman screaming something is always the easiest for you all to enjoy. I know your famous sister did.

But Gary Oldman should have called for an ambulance himself in advance with the latest pesonal technology that he was shooting a commercial for.

But Gary Oldman should have had his hand held at the hospital by an ur-friend keeping solemn vigil until he succumbs from his grievous injuries.

But Gary Oldman should have become the unlikeliest perfect incorruptable vessel of human salvation sent by geedee to lead our spiritual revolution against all that oppresses us.

Yes yes yes, there should be something more to see, you all insist, unaware that Gary Oldman knows better than all of you. He does so wish he could be that gentle person to guide all the other gentle people along past what is nearest and dearest to you all, but he can't help himself for only watching instead. It is only another day for everyone else. Yet the sunrise he watches on the rooftop returns to him as I have believed it will: this someone who he would see in himself, who did not deserve to die in front of him though he knows her from a glimpse in a mirror he did not take, a walk through a neighborhood he had never been in, a door he did not hold open but opened all the same with an eagerness he recognized from somewhere else, a different day that occurs to him.

Would you care if I didn't, he asks her

because he can only ask when it is not another day, as evidenced by her shabby presence. No one else watching these two. Everyone is asleep, dreaming of the latest personal technology he had desired putting into their hands, pining for another Gary Oldman who could be young enough not to care again about plate-glass doors and grievous injuries, before they have to go to their respective buidlings for the day. From atop a building, a voice calls out what is left of that desire he had known as belonging to someone else until it became his own, until it succeeded him, until he lost it by listening to it. A voice leaves him standing alone with her on the rooftop, watching her extend an AUTOGRAPHS book with pen for him to take. Another curse is dangling unlit from his lips.

EPILOGUE:
YOU AND YOU ALL CAN NEVER HAVE ENOUGH EPILOGUES

THERE IS A PERSON you see

so this person is not altogether unfamiliar to you, as familiarity here is only contingent upon sight itself. It is possible your days and weeks and months at the social building have given you some exposure to the fancies of a secret admirer willing to narrate various circumstances of occurring preceded by small talk and the usual banality of amusing incidents already creating an alternative history in this person's mind of such gentility that came about. The privileging of self is something you have already come to expect in your dealings with people in the aberrant, self-loathing city. Let it happen, you think, and perhaps someone will amuse or entertain you with an anecdote. You haven't had a good one in awhile, it suddenly occurs to you, you shuddering at considering this self-narrated, clichéd *suddenly*

so this person suddenly asks while you sit in your lame cubicle, Does anyone know this person, with *person* substituted for an aforementioned specific name familiar to you, like any name, perhaps, and this other person seeking any sort of sudden confirmation from a face—especially yours, for some reason—suddenly realizes there is no help coming at all to ascertain this confirmation of identity which, in a social building, is a terrible disappointment suddenly afflicting this person. You would like to explain any name will elide itself in a hearer's memory for this *suddenly* it possesses, this instructive moment, where possession, interpretation, but not decision comes into play. No one knows this person if not for *suddenly*; without it, such a person is as good as gone, implied as it already is when someone asks you, in this particular building, if you happen to know this person. The anecdote which follows never brings a smile to your face. Another day in the social building suddenly taking place.

In a building, any building, every building, you and you all are always studious creatures looking for explanations from the fellow and the like. The process always makes someone nervous, which is why it is often very difficult to care about alternative history studies. Do this for me, is plead. Tell me of that, is pined. Be gentle with those, is deferred. What is really being dealt with here, will be asked if not presented the facts. No. Meaning yourselves owed. Suggesting another though is not another in mind. Given Time to think of one should the building allow, which, of course, it doesn't. Can't. Won't. There is no difference. Down the hallway, to the left. First door you see. You take another door you don't see instead. Can't. Won't. But you know you are still in the building. How can you not. The outside you once imagined is the imagination you leave behind for good, and no door will take you back there no matter how far down the hallway you travel thinking of a particular someone you traveled with, however briefly, who knew a thing or two of hallways, who kept you company, showed you the door when you were ready to quit the building.

So to no one in particular: I quit, you say.

A distinct advantage of quitting is that you have much more Time for other people you would prefer to spend Time with, such as the gentle man who narrates himself as Gary Oldman in your latest exorbitant cohabitation scheme.

Gentle people like to say gaining Time is the only real advantage to be had in this world. You'll get over it, then. You tried and tried, and you quit. You lost. You lost your famous sister. You lost her purse with the AUTOGRAPHS book during the move. You lost sleep. You lost a somewhat decent exorbitant cohabitation scheme prior to this new one. You lost a hypothetical unpublished translated novel by Maurice Blanchot of indeterminate monetary and literary value. You lost the black boy (something of a loss). You lost your sad upstairs neighbor who kept monopolizing the laundry machines (no great loss). You lost your security deposit (a great loss indeed). You even lost your water for a little while, unable to take those hot baths you enjoy so much. In all, this is plenty to lose. It is not everything you can think of right now, to be sure, nor is it everything important, though it does feel like everything to you. Such is the nature of loss in the aberrant, self-loathing city without so much as a single anecdote to hang your proverbial hat on, unless an ur-friend keeps patient wait to make you forget it all on a daily basis.

You had looked for such a gentle person in your midst not long after your quitting, walking home through the jumbly neighborhoods, taking the beaten subway to nowhere in particular, consulting the more stylish literary periodicals at the depressed public library, or imbibing in silence your new favorite blend of coffee at your favorite chain coffee shop to pass the Time but not celebrate it. You watched the first snow of winter fall and thought of a certain story you had enjoyed set in a far away land—though not too far away—where a gentle man who wants very much to remain a gentle man is watching the snow fall while thinking of what his gentle wife is thinking, namely, of a very gentle young man who had grown ill and died because of his standing in that same snow many years ago, she tells him, while waiting for her to do something gentle, who his gentle wife had once loved. Soon this gentle husband who wants very much to remain a gentle man has an epiphany. He realizes he has been living in an exorbitant cohabitation scheme with a stealthy adolescent romantic ur-friend all these years, courtesy of his gentle wife, and never was he aware of it until just now with the snow falling. Then he quits, albeit in the gentlest way possible. He quits because the snow falls on everyone, there, not there, who cares. This is the measure of his gentleness, he sees, since he can observe its ruination, covering and covered as it does. This world loves its dead lovers so. Why should he be any different, he thinks. He sees he is not touching his gentle wife in any way whatsoever or looking into her eyes. She is crying as you were crying, but you were not crying for her, not for him, not even for the stealthy adolescent romantic ur-friend in his paltry winter attire. You were crying because some exorbitant cohabitation schemes are better than others, such as the ones the snow does not fall upon since some people are neither living nor dead, but merely waiting patient somewhere for someone to arrive and leave with them, should leaving be a possibility granted.

You yourself would very much like to leave this aberrant, self-loathing city. For good. Yet it is always difficult to know where to go next without the proper guidance. There should be an ending for the ending, you insist, an epilogue to suggest a correct path or any available one. Something should be added to fool you into believing it is never over when you know it really is, like *Sid and Nancy*. Someone has to show the way who is not actually there. For instance, Sid Vicious leaves with Nancy Spungen in a driverless taxi cab into what you think is the afterlife reunion, and this non-existent taxi driver has to hang around and watch it all. No one ever thinks about the non-existent taxi driver in *Sid and Nancy*. He can leave for anywhere he wants to, but he can't. Too busy driving gentle and not-so-gentle people through the snow. Too busy thinking about when his non-existent day will end so he can put his feet up and watch television. Too busy chatting up his rides about failed exorbitant cohabitation schemes. This one, he stabbed me, see. Shrugs. Whattaya gonna do, I love him and he loves me, too. That's great, that's great. Looks out the window. Snow keeps falling. Fare adds up. No one is crying anymore. No one is thinking about stealthy adolescent romantics (unless they were one themselves). All thoughts are preoccupied by snow. Snow preoccupies you. Thinking you seldom see it when you leave for anywhere, you step out and away. You are leaving, only going so far, however, as to your next exorbitant cohabitation scheme with a full bag of groceries in your arms, where you know the gentle man who narrates himself as Gary Oldman, the big quitter, the biggest quitter of them all, will be waiting for you suddenly on your next sofa.

The gentle man who narrates himself as Gary Oldman has come along into your life and decided to stick around to make amends for its evident shortcomings. For everything, that is. He's very gentle, you think while admiring his voice. He wants to talk to you. Personally. Heart-to-heart. He needs to tell you about how Gary Oldman could have been considered for the role of Travis Bickle in Martin Scorsese's *Taxi Driver* by his meeting with the director in the lobby of the famous Hotel Chelsea if not for a trivial intercession of anecdotal behavior.

The reasons for the gentle man who narrates himself as Gary Oldman wanting this—long and convoluted as they may be for an epilogue—are constructed for an epilogue amended, as it were, to the remaining narrative which had thought itself finished with the dispatching of important thematic content and its principle figures feeling screwed over on some plane of recognition but acknowledging silently the Time to move on by not really moving on but ending, which they can't actually acknowledge because no one does in an ending, the lone exception being Chloe Webb as Nancy Spungen in *Sid and Nancy* as she looks into a bathroom mirror at the Hotel Chelsea the moment she will die, only to be, for lack of a more fitting paradigm, reincarnated as the vestigial virgin for the whiter shade of pale afterlife reunion with Gary Oldman as the Sid Vicious who will never be entirely dead yet, as least as a throng of appreciative black boys listening to disco on a boombox would have it. This, in the history of modern American cinema, would constitute in its evident perfection the epilogue-in-itself, defying all convention and causality that the life of Sid Vicious represents. The viewer would remember all this if not for the substituting authority of the violent alcoholism of Gary Oldman, however, leaving other filmmakers like Luis Buñuel to fume in his Simonist tomb for being born fifty years too early, before there was such a thing to his knowledge as a sex pistol. The right tool for the right job. Some are fortunate. Maybe even lucky. The rest get a standard epilogue like a cheap funeral. *Fin.*

This is all quite delicious, Gary Oldman will think many years later, finally enjoying himself after decades of pointless jetsetting. No more fucking commercial shoots for me, yeah. Take up writing a story collection instead. *Twenty-Two Epilogues for Twenty-One Centuries.* Why twenty-two. You'll just have to plunk down your thirty hardcover bucks and find out yourself, love.

He can already see the epilogue he will write.

If there is anyone capable to make the world care about epilogues again, it's him, Gary Oldman will determine, with some additional prodding by his hairless agent, looking up his connections at the New York publishing houses to stir some interest up. Gary, you could start with that loon at the Gehry last year. Always need a violent incident to start with. Shock to the system sort of deal. Everything's *in media res* now, anyway, no exposition. The pang of childbirth, the torture of existence, and what follows. What's an epilogue for all that. Love it. No one's going to see this coming. Need a place to write this. Get away for awhile. How about an upstate residency. Fill a room with pages. Fill the world with epilogues. Can think of at least a dozen others who'll do it if you don't. You're going to let them have all the fun. Take all the glory.

Someone will, that you can count on, Gary Oldman grouses to himself, I know I have. Not even my bleeding hairless agent talks me out of it. Someone picks up where you left off. Someone carries your gentle body out the door where no one ever sees it again. All the loving memory in the world won't make it less easy. If anything, someone'll wish they did it sooner. Couldn't hurt, yeah.

Gary Oldman is so not intent to star in a film by this Scorsese bloke or play a nutter like Travis Bickle, regardless of how much this character appeals to him upon reading the script despite Bickle's lack of alcoholic tendencies. Meeting someone at the famous Hotel Chelsea when he is not famous, not Sid Vicious, not anyone, really, not even Gary Oldman, could be beneficial to his career since all gentle people are disdainful of him and the subtle obscenity of his physicality whose whiteness knows no bounds because there is nothing in his life—which he stubbornly accepts. This preference of his own painful whiteness, as thin a pretense as any to meet Martin Scorsese face-to-face in New York, would not serve much anecdotal value in the aberrant, self-loathing city, to be sure, though that's hardly the point, a gentle man who narrates himself as Gary Oldman tells you. What is the point, Gary Oldman wonders. He finds the seat offered to him in the lobby of the famous Hotel Chelsea to have a spring dislodged somewhere near his backside in a very inopportune place under a layer of faux-pleather. He has to shift himself as Scorsese starts talking about, of all things, London, confessing he has never been there, would like to go scout Whitechapel for a Ripper flick he had always considered doing while at film school but doesn't have the script yet, all the while Gary Oldman noticing, while lifting his right arm to prop his head, a small spot on the armrest where his hand just was. A small red spot he indentifies immediately but squints his eyes at it all the same, finding a thumb-print in blood, dried well into the faux-pleather and leaving a full outline of the whorl in the center. Scorsese, not noticing this, tells Gary Oldman that though he is worried about the British accent he would like to try on a Travis with beady eyes and a receding chin. He scans Oldman's willingness to bulk up a bit since Bickle is an ex-Marine, to try going without sleep for three-day intervals, develop a high threshold for physical pain, learn how to improvise dialogue while mock-shooting a gun at a mirror, get familiar with the Times Square porno theater circuit, subsist on a steady diet of only Big Macs, Doritos, Hostess cupcakes, RC Cola and stale jujubes, and phone him at the end of the month in Bickle's character. Gary Oldman, distracted momentarily from the bloody thumb-print, does not care much for the ad-libbing request—goes against his training. Real emotion can't be dramatic while conveyed impromptu but needs to be built up to a pre-determined moment and then released. Boom. Otherwise it's too jumbly, as he puts it. Scorsese counters, Hey that's ok that's ok, Gary, Travis is a jumbly guy, see, not Oedipus but something like Oedipus he's trying to solve the riddle of this life, this diseased, decaying cursed city, and he'll do whatever he has to wash the streets clean, of course it's too much for him to bear because he thought he bore it all, served his country, now look at him, nothing but No-Doz and cafeteria pie and watching it all night after night, ready for someone to stick a .45 in his neck and telling him to fork it over or you're dead motherfucker you're dead—but he can't be dead until he puts it right, see, no one's allowed to kill him. You can't kill the king. Can't get uppity with him, either. So Travis is going to set it right regardless of what it does to him, going to follow that incestuous truth towards whatever inevitability gouges his eyes out at the end—Iris. The girl he doesn't know what to do with, but save her. Maybe he will. Maybe he saves everyone. In the process though he can't save himself—and that's the idea, the idea of, no the *reality* of contemporary life, *city* life, see, city life is all a jumble, spontaneous passions, but solve the riddle, leave the city—maimed, blinded, fucked—but he ain't leaving, you see. He can never leave—

all the while his animated explanation getting more and more animated with his wild gesticulations growing more and more wild as the other guests in the lobby ignore them both with more and more seething intensity because this is New York your narrator is talking about,

until, put off by Scorsese's interminable rambling, Gary Oldman turns his weary head. He notices someone. No one else would have at that particular moment, as this is someone not inclined to longwinded diatribes or trying to make sense. This not-so gentle person blows through the lobby entrance, failing to hold the door open for, presumably, his addict girlfriend stumbling along in tow while he hails a taxi and barrels into it with her in a matter of seconds employing a breathtaking fluidity of garbled motion and the flaunting of failed etiquette, at least by Gary Oldman's internal clock. The girlfriend somehow finds her way into the back of the taxi with him without so much as a single finger lifted in her assistance, nearly catching her own foot in the closing door as the someone Gary Oldman notices sits quietly, passively in the back as though he could sit in that spot forever.

Before the taxi does speed off with its eventual destination given but not perceived, Gary Oldman studies the non-existent driver from whatever best vantage the filmy glass window pane in the Hotel Chelsea lobby affords him with Scorsese still making his case in his left ear. Gary Oldman can't help noting the non-existent taxi driver never turns his head to meet the faces of his occupants, never turning—a mistake he himself has just made thinking he knows the couple—since, he sees, it is not important to see the faces without the mirror. The mirror is everything, even the turning itself. Transport, commerce involving, observation pertaining to, social etiquette (or further observation), two coins for the trouble, eh. Toss toss. That's all. Systematic reduction on a more or less Cartesian grid of streets and neighborhoods and dingy hotels like this one. A bloody thumb-print is all that is takes to leave it, the notion occurs to Gary Oldman, because no one comes around to wash it clean but the non-existent taxi driver. Because he does not have to look directly at it. Gary Oldman watches the non-existent taxi driver adjust the rear view with more than a tinge of jealousy as the someone he knew finally says something, the non-existent taxi driver puts the taxi into motion, and off they all go, certain that he will never see the couple again in the particular moment as he has witnessed them occurring with a bloody thumb-print, as it was, while, at the same moment, remembering he is sitting in a faux-pleather chair with Martin Scorsese in front of him, still talking away to someone if not a Gary Oldman who does not speak a further word out of fear

of a suddenly Gary Oldman who would stand up from his faux-pleather chair with a spot of dried blood on his right index finger which Scorsese may notice immediately and suddenly interrupt himself to say, Hey you all right Gary—but this suddenly Gary Oldman may have already bailed for the lobby door where another taxi will suddenly pull up as if it were hailed, though it won't be.

Two days later, Robert DeNiro gets a call.

Not for a lack of effort in this exorbitant cohabitation scheme, you will later imagine just enough the gentle man who narrates himself as Gary Oldman trying to explain without fear this hypothetical fear Gary Oldman would have experienced, and doing so under the most banal of circumstances to be rendered anecdotally.

Your narrator takes a chance, he would tell you if he was here right now with you, with what you may presume to be a sympathetic, intelligent, but not condescending gentle man at a bar during a typical, anecdotal chance encounter. The two are complete strangers to each other, of course, and they make an unspoken pact to remain as such because of the bar's public confines, or in spite of them. The gentle man, prodded on by successive drinks, grew attentive as your narrator spoke. Soon growing eager. Soon willing to explore his deepest, most intimate narratological inhibitions down to the last draw from his glass his throat can take. Your narrator feels both pleased and his audience's pleasure. There is a perfect reciprocity of etiquette. Your narrator forgets about you, that it happens to be your birthday tonight, his responsibilities to you and the current exorbitant cohabitation scheme and your waiting impatiently for him somewhere this evening to celebrate whatever about your birthday needs celebrating. Naturally, overconfidently, but not intentionally, he makes a gross mistake, a terrible slip of reasoning. He starts talking to his audience about the importance of Gary Oldman.

Your narrator in his inexperience fails to explain to his audience who is shifting uncomfortably upon his tattered bar stool, as a Time-honored aside, how a flawed obsession with the violent alcoholic acting style of Gary Oldman finds its match occurring with a someone else no less than your famous sister to everyone else, a fame not having been based upon reason or logic or archetype or even a near-academic study worthy of any cinema scholar but a slow, steady succumbing to the idea of Gary Oldman from her nearly playing Nancy Spungen in the 1986 film *Sid and Nancy* instead of Chloe Webb. Then, as he understands it, she nearly succumbed to Gary Oldman a second Time, though in much more anecdotal fashion—or, at least, your narrator thinks so. He knows more than a few anecdotes about her which may put a certain fear into Gary Oldman and not resemble any anecdote from his own violent alcoholic life filled with entertainment or edification or both but resemble instead a few choice scenes from *Sid and Nancy* not making the final cut: alley jumpings, throat slashings, pub glassings, Chelsea smiles, actual automatic gunfire, kittens getting flushed down toilets, prolonged tortured screams in the endless night. These are the sort of turmoil items someone like Gary Oldman shares a certain intimacy with, not unlike your narrator's intimacy with your famous sister if not you and you all. And with all this intimacy abounding, your narrator keeps tally of the number of occasions that anyone may bother to ask him, Are you Gary Oldman, to which he would reply hurriedly, intently, but not interestedly, No, no I'm not.

Because, as your narrator further fails to explain to the drunken gentle man who quits him suddenly without a word and leaves the bar, it's not interesting being a Gary Oldman to everyone only interested in the anecdotal Gary Oldman who flits through the haunts of Los Angeles as if they are a Gehry Museum which exists only in his mind for a single gentle person. Who would dare not only profess interest in him but make him an ur-friend unto perpetuity so that one may never face the afterlife reunion alone—much like how Gary Oldman as Sid Vicious faces it for awhile—the catch being Nancy Spungen does show up, a Nancy Spungen who was played by Chloe Webb and not your famous sister. Thus leaves your famous sister in the impossible caesura of waiting and not-waiting should she reach out her hand to Gary Oldman with her AUTOGRAPHS book and pen and say, I nearly, like, worked with you on *Sid and Nancy*. She knows she cannot say this to him, nor will she ever say this, as she languishes in Los Angeles for a chance, indefinite as it may be, to prove the existence of the Gehry Museum outside the mind of a Gary Oldman, a someone else who has already been everyone else he can possibly be somewhere in Los Angeles. Gary Oldman needs a narrator to make him someone else again to your famous sister, to give him another day so he can be a famous tortured composer, an intergalactic weapons trader, a post-apocalyptic warlord, an unfortunate Rastafarian. Of course, your famous sister will never see these colorful roles for herself. His fame is far too great to scale without someone else who knows and shares the vicissitudes of this day and an undying appreciation for *Sid and Nancy* from having watched it over and over at the leisure of a Gary Oldman inside the television who would never be able to find his own face in a crowd.

This conversation without a fellow required conversant lasts into the early hours of the morning, your narrator going it alone until well past Quitting

Time. The bar has cleared out. Everyone has left, bartender included.

So to no one in particular: I had this coming, your narrator says.

For a long while the silent insult stings. Since everyone in the bar leaves when they shouldn't, the gentle man who narrates himself as Gary Oldman will struggle to comprehend the larger non-spoken rebuke on either a personal or intellectual level in relation to your likely growing anger about him missing your birthday because of a barroom conversation with a complete stranger, one-sided as it may have been.

During this darkest night, abandoned by his audience all because of Gary Oldman, he wanders in abject misery through all the immortal boroughs looking for you, needing you, not unlike a certain Italian gentle man long ago insofar as his mid-life crisis desperately needed some company to survive the greatest insult the world had heaped upon him. To be cast aside so mercilessly, even in the capacity as a narrator which he would serve for the gentle man in the bar and does serve here for you now, is indeed a dire circumstance and judgment passed upon a person in this life which needs as many facts as possible, and, by inference, far less fiction to be deluded with. If the matter were political, the gentle man listening could have merely accused the narrator of being Orwellian. If vulgar, a simple snorting at him of, Bullshit, and be done with it. But it is different when one is a source of authority where none can be found. This frightens the gentle man who narrates himself as Gary Oldman. Are narrators allowed to be frightened. Don't they narrate to pre-empt that fear to some degree. They may say they are fearful, yes, imply something to suggest they are frightened, wounded even, but isn't there enough detachment in any story, near or far, to reconcile it.

Narrators who narrate themselves as Gary Oldman don't fear. Anecdotes about Gary Oldman don't die.

Throughout Time, the gentle man who narrates himself as Gary Oldman will tell you, gentle men have dispensed and returned more insults upon the world than those who are not gentle, and better than Gary Oldman ever could. He will say this no longer your narrator now, but someone else's if not his own, a someone else as of yet unidentified but soon to be found somewhere, in some level, in some story. In this capacity here, wandering through these neighborhoods looking for you on your day of birth, your narrator is a lowly facsimile of such gentle men, his kenosis on display for all to see for telling tales of woe and the strangely reassuring ice waiting for you and him at the lowest level—*that*, he remembers at least, was the part which intrigued you in your upstate high school when you and your famous sister were living with your civil servant parents. Those who were the least gentle with their Time consign your other narrators to touch the ice with their feet so they may look upon the administrator of din with a certain approbation of guiltlessness. There in the gesture you saw it: Hell is what makes its own truth continually, viciously, but not attractively, unless it is tread upon with the numbness you and you all could expect from two Italian gentle men wearing leather sandals. The fact of Hell—which serves no fact in of itself—can be killed by the simplest of gestures, the most innocent of anecdotal conversations, if only so it could be conquered by a narrator. Though it may still be a blatant falsehood when the deed is done, your narrator understands, there is no world but the one gentle people create without gentleness, and that will be enough for them to inhabit it. The facts, meanwhile, forever wait patient, and thus beautiful.

Complete utter Orwellian bullshit, a gentle person your narrator narrates says.

A touching reunion anecdote for all the gentle people, then.

When the gentle man who narrates himself as Gary Oldman finds you alone at a late-night greasy pizza stand you had frequented with someone you once knew from a prior exorbitant cohabitation scheme, with you not eating anything at present and voluminous tears in your eyes, he is ready to talk about something more important than Gary Oldman, but only if you are ready to listen.

All that this role frightens him the most: he wants to explain himself. He really does. It's not because of the mostly anecdotal things about you and your famous sister he has learned and will have to narrate in some way later. It's something far worse since, among other reasons, he fears he may bore the Hell out of everyone because he has done so already, and may have to do it again and again. His trite narrative language can't be anything less than entertaining or edifying or both after tonight. You have been down this road before, to be sure. Will you quit him. Will you point at him, perhaps laugh at his obsolescence. Will you take pity instead since your narrator can't possibly know better. Will you quit yourself.

As a belated birthday gift, your narrator shows you the futility of his own truth to help you make your final decision. He gently takes you by the shoulders and walks you back home through the jumbly neighborhoods as though you and he are intruders here. In a way, you both are. Will forever be. There is a black boy following you both, pointing and laughing, understanding this well. He does not have a predictable boom box in hand but flails wildly a typewritten manuscript, and the disbelieving looks of those you pass by are the accompanying portraiture, those who are also pointing and laughing— with the exception of one sad countenance whose face is lost as a gust of wind pushes her yellowing white hair over it. Because, the gentle man who narrates himself as Gary Oldman explains to you, he does not want all of them joyous or recognizable. Disbelievers are not bought or sold here. He is not selling them, or himself. They are mere faces framed unto their own grace delayed or the lack, perpetually left to themselves. You look upon these faces as you walk by, all gathering, all gathered. You both are willing intruders to them so your feet may touch the ice, so you may never have to touch the ice again afterwards. Or so you dare hope.

The gentle man who narrates himself as Gary Oldman confesses as you arrive with him at the building where you currently pay exorbitant rent for very little in return. He wants them all to be in this building, your building, and you will never leave them, these gentle people who laugh at him, at you, at your famous sister, everything. Go back inside, he will tell you and them while pointing at the door, annoyed in that Gary Oldman way. He doesn't want you or anyone else to leave. His way will be that which keeps you and them in there, where all gathered are speaking a story not your own, not belonging to any other narrator. It has been he who must narrate what comes next, he who says

I could sell you ice in Hell, you all.

ACKNOWLEDGMENTS

Many thanks to the editors of *alice blue review, Anomalous, The Collagist, Heavy Feather Review, theNewerYork* (on-line), *Black Sun Lit* and *Vestiges* where selections originally appeared; to the editors of Noemi Press for naming this manuscript a semi-finalist for their 2015 Book Contest in Fiction; to my friends and colleagues at Marshall University's Department of English, as well as all those who have supported me over the years; to everyone at What Books; and to Gary.

FORREST ROTH'S work has appeared in *NOON*, *Denver Quarterly*, *Juked*, *Caketrain*, *The Collagist*, and other journals. He is also the author of a novella, *Line and Pause* (BlazeVOX Books), and a prose poem chapbook, *The Sullen Pages* (Little Red Leaves). He received his Creative Writing Ph.D. from the University of Louisiana at Lafayette, and is a Visiting Assistant Professor of English at Marshall University in West Virginia.

WHAT
BOOKS
PRESS

LOS ANGELES

TITLES FROM
WHAT BOOKS PRESS

POETRY

Molly Bendall & Gail Wronsky, *Bling & Fringe (The L.A. Poems)*

Laurie Blauner, *It Looks Worse Than I Am*

Kevin Cantwell, *One of Those Russian Novels*

Ramón García, *Other Countries*

Karen Kevorkian, *Lizard Dream*

Holaday Mason & Sarah Maclay, *The "She" Series: A Venice Correspondence*

Carolie Parker, *Mirage Industry*

Patty Seyburn, *Perfecta*

Judith Taylor, *Sex Libris*

Lynne Thompson, *Start with a Small Guitar*

Gail Wronsky, *Imperfect Pastorals*

Gail Wronsky, *So Quick Bright Things*
BILINGUAL, SPANISH TRANSLATED BY ALICIA PARTNOY

ART

Gronk, *A Giant Claw*
BILINGUAL, SPANISH

Chuck Rosenthal, Gail Wronsky & Gronk,
Tomorrow You'll Be One of Us: Sci Fi Poems

What Books Press books may be ordered from:

SPDBOOKS.ORG | ORDERS@SPDBOOKS.ORG | (800) 869 7553 | AMAZON.COM

Visit our website at

WHATBOOKSPRESS.COM

www.ingramcontent.com/pod-product-compliance
Lightning Source LLC
Chambersburg PA
CBHW021020120726
47905CB00009B/3099